JOINING UP

JOINING UP
Tom Gray

Cover Artwork © 1889 Books 2021
Image of couple in the garden courtesy
of the collection of Maureen Kay
Title font: Umbrage – thanks to Vic Fieger

www.1889books.co.uk

ISBN: 978-1-9163622-8-4

For Susan

Foreword

My Grandfather, William John Farrow, volunteered to serve his country and was awarded the Military Medal for an act of bravery during the battle of the Somme. As an inquisitive child, I wanted to ask him about what he did to be awarded the medal, but my mother always insisted that I shouldn't ever raise the subject and so William's war time experiences died with him.

The inspiration for this novel came both from my Grandad's untold story and after learning how so many young men from my own city of Sheffield volunteered to serve and made the ultimate sacrifice. I have attempted to be as accurate as possible, with regards to the events leading up to July the first 1916 and I believe that the description of the battle itself is very close to what happened on that day.

The narrative is intended to represent the experiences of many in this city, whose lives were shaped by war and who bore the scars for the rest of their lives. I honour them.

Chapter One

'Christmas tree, sweaty old trainers, golf clubs... ah, here it is... Matthew, hold this will you?'

Dad's hands appeared from up inside the loft hatch, holding a square wooden box, with what looked like a hundred years worth of dust resting on it.

'Dad! It's got cobwebs and all sorts on it.'

'Just get it please,' said Dad, 'I'll give it a wipe when I'm out of this dreadful place.'

Dad's long legs emerged and, after some grunting and straining, he was eventually back on solid ground. In the beams of sunlight, coming through the landing window, I could see the cloud of dust from the loft drifting gently around in the still air of the landing.

'Let's get it outside and have a look inside, shall we?'

I followed him outside into the garden and, with the box between us, we sat cross-legged on the lawn as he began to carefully lift out the contents and lay them on an old sheet.

I remember some bundles of envelopes, each with an address written in spidery handwriting. There was also something that he was sure was an old army cap-badge and some faded photographs of young men smiling and posing in military uniform, next to a large gun.

Through his glasses, I noticed that a tear was running down dad's cheek, so I looked away, until he'd wiped it away. He was always embarrassed to be seen to be showing emotion.

'Your Granddad brought you up, didn't he?'

'That's right. After our parents were killed, he and Grandma became what they call the legal guardians of my sister and me; meaning that they became our parents.'

Dad rarely mentioned his childhood and so I decided to take the opportunity to find out more about it. He told me that he was only a baby when his parents had died and that he had no memories of them.

'Is that your Granddad on that photograph?' I asked.

'Yes, that's him in the middle. I'd recognise that smile anywhere. He looks happy doesn't he? I reckon that's his older brother, standing next to him; you can tell that they're brothers. Let's see what's it says on the back?'

Dad screwed up his face in an effort to read the faded handwriting on the reverse side,

'It says… wait a minute, it's a bit faint… Ah yes… My pals… the Sheffield City Battalion of the York and Lancs. Regiment. I think can just about make out some names… Boulby… Wortley… Long… and I'm sure that says "Our Joe." It's all such a pity.'

'What's a pity, Dad?'

'I always wonder about each of these men, what's their story? What did they do out there? I don't suppose we'll ever know. Then there's my Granddad's medal… I often wonder what happened to that.'

'What medal did they give him?'

'I'm pretty sure it was the Military Medal, which is one of the highest medals they give for bravery. You've got to do something really brave to earn it, but as with everything to do with the war, Granddad never talked about it.'

'Didn't you ever ask him?'

'No, not really. In fact, I was always encouraged not to talk about it, because he'd had seen some awful things and really didn't want to re-live them. Of course, I knew bits and pieces here and there, such as his older brother being killed and various cousins not coming home again, but I'm sorry to say that his war died with him. Anyway, mum and Amanda will be home soon, so we'd better look like we've done something while they've been out. You start doing the washing up and I'll get the Hoover on the stairs and try to get rid of some of that dust.'

Amanda was my older sister. She was thirteen at the time and she suffered from both autism and severe epileptic seizures. Mum had taken her out somewhere, for what we called, "a change of air." What that actually meant, was that Amanda was probably becoming anxious, because of some small change in routine or an unexpected minor event, which to others would be of no importance.

Amanda's epilepsy often resulted in seizures lasting several minutes and involved a loss of consciousness, stiffening and shaking. As with her autism, my parents and I were aware of what to do in an emergency. We knew not to try and restrain her and to guide her gently away from dangers, like a busy road. We always talked to her calmly and reassuringly, so as not to cause her to become anxious.

Later that day, when Amanda was upstairs listening to music, my parents and I were playing Scrabble at the dining room table, when dad asked where Mum and Amanda had been.

'Well, you know what she's like,' said Mum, 'she gets these ideas in her head and won't give up until she's done it.'

'So what happened?'

'We were standing in Pond Street bus station, trying to decide where to go, when she started begging me to let her get the number 16 bus. I tried to get her to tell me why she wanted to ride on that one, but she just insisted that we get on. She was making such as fuss that I gave up and we got on anyway.'

Dad looked up from the Scrabble board and laughed, asking, 'So where did you end up?'

'It was quite nice actually. We went up Loxley Hill and got off at the top. The views across the countryside from up there are lovely and there were some horses that came over to the farm gate to say "hello." She spent ages stroking and talking to them, and for a while she was really happy. We must have stayed there for at least an hour, before deciding to walk back down towards Hillsborough. The funny thing is…'

'What?'

'Nothing really… I got had the strangest sense that she knew that part of town very well. She was telling me about who lived in this house and who lived in that house and how Bill used to walk up the hill to see… I can't remember who exactly. Then, would you believe it, she wanted to go to Attercliffe.'

'Why on earth?'

'You tell me. Anyway, we caught another bus and had a look at some of the steelworks and she seemed to enjoy that as much as the countryside. I think she'll sleep well tonight; I will for sure!'

Chapter Two

I was ten years old, and in my final year in primary school. Our drama teacher Miss Tuke had cast me in the lead role in a short play that she'd written about the war. I played the part of a soldier coming home to his parents and reminiscing about life in the trenches. Lucy Oram played the role of my mum and most of the class had lines to say or sing. "Keep The Home Fires Burning," as the play was called, was performed on November the Eleventh, in front of our parents and other guests. I remember we sang "We'll Meet Again" in front of a large union flag and that poppies were scattered from above the stage, rather like they are at the Royal Albert Hall.

Afterwards, Mrs Hodgson, the Headteacher thanked everyone involved in putting on the show, and after that we mingled around in the hall, being congratulated by our parents and in some cases, grandparents. That is when I met Mr Spears.

I had seen him before at other school functions and I knew that he was a resident at The Ferns which was a care home located next to the school. The kids had sometimes gone there at Christmas time to sing them carols, so it was no surprise to see some of them at our show. On this particular day, Mr Spears was sitting alone in his wheelchair, seemingly deep in thought. He was a large man, with a shock of white hair and steel blue eyes. He was wearing a smart blue blazer, on which a military crest was embroidered on the handkerchief pocket. His tie was ramrod straight and bore the same insignia as that on his blazer.

'Hello,' I said as I approached him and he turned to face me. As we shook hands, I noticed that he was missing the tips of several fingers.

'That was really good,' he said. 'Made my day has that. I can't see much these days, but that didn't stop me enjoying it. You were the main bloke in it, weren't you?'

'Yes.' And without hesitation, I asked, 'Were you in the First World War?'

'Aye, I was. My goodness me, it seems like it was a thousand years ago… all those young lads who didn't make it home. I dunno. Anyway, are you going to join the army one day?'

'I don't know. I might do.'

'Well don't! It's bloody horrible! I lost many of my mates in the first lot. That's why I wear this badge. It's to remember them and not just to celebrate winning a war. If only young folk today knew what we went through… I'm sorry… I get carried away sometimes.'

'My dad's Granddad was in that war.'

'You mean your Great-Granddad? Crikey that makes me feel very old. What was his name? Was he from these parts?'

Suddenly and with a terrible feeling of embarrassment, I realised that I couldn't answer either of these questions.

'I'm not sure exactly, I'll go and ask my dad… '

'George, come on love, it's time for a cuppa before bed-time.' Before I could ask Dad, a young man from the care home had arrived and started to push Mr Spears towards the door and back to The Ferns.

I thought about running after him and trying to learn more about his experiences, but he was whisked away so quickly that it was impossible.

Chapter Three

Let's be honest, most lessons at school are instantly forgettable, but on this particular day instead of Mr Pannick's usual lesson we had a visitor from the local museum, who had brought along some exhibits for us to look at and handle. Much to my delight, the museum lady had brought some genuine recruitment posters from the First World War. Some had Lord Kitchener pointing and saying that "Your Country Needs You!" Another poster was of a woman looking proudly through a window as some young British soldiers marched past her house on their way to war. By far the most interesting thing was a collection of shells and bullets, brought home by some soldiers at the end of the war. They had been made safe, but just to hold them and imagine loading them into a gun before actually firing them was the highlight of my day, and I couldn't wait to tell my parents about it.

My excitement was brought to an end, as soon as opened the front door and went inside. Immediately, I could hear Amanda screaming and I knew and mum was clearly struggling. I dumped my school bag and went into the living room where I was faced with Amanda holding a vase of flowers and threatening to throw it through the window. Mum had positioned herself between Amanda and the window and was trying to calm her down by singing a Beatles song. Mum knew that Amanda was close to being obsessed by the Beatles and that their music often calmed her down; but on this occasion, she was having a hard time and even the "Fab Four" were not having their usual tranquillising effect on Amanda. We'd been in this situation many times and I'd had some training on what to do, so, quietly, I began to talk to Amanda about some of the fun things that we might do together, including listening to some music or she could tell me about Sergeant Pepper's Lonely Hearts Club Band.

Amanda eventually put down the vase and was soon sitting next to me, chatting about Ringo Starr, as if this had never happened. She was highly intelligent and very articulate, particularly in matters relating to the Beatles and the 1960s; in fact I've often said that if she were on Mastermind, she would answer every question correctly. Her autism meant that she had problems with any change in routine and the disturbance of the daily pattern of events. If something unusual happened, it might send Amanda into a very disturbed state of mind and she could become extremely emotional and sometimes aggressive. Even a sudden noise or a light bulb going out, could cause her to become upset and I could see the strain that her condition placed on Mum and Dad.

Sometimes Amanda's autism would cause us all to collapse into gales of laughter. On one occasion, she asked a woman, who was waiting behind us in the queue in Morrisons, why she had such a big nose and she once led a sing-along on the bus home from town. A lot of the time, however, her autism took it out on my parents and getting up at two a.m. on most nights to change the wet bedclothes of a teenager is tough.

Eventually, the strain on mum became too much and her health began to suffer. She'd battled through the winter, when Amanda spent most of her time indoors, but by springtime, mum needed a break. Dad arranged to take some time off work, but even that wasn't enough to allow her to recover her strength. She was buckling under the strain. Amanda's special school were very helpful and arranged for her to spend a week in a residential centre for young people with various types of special needs. The respite centre was thirty miles away, somewhere near Leeds. Dad used to drive her there and he said that he always found it difficult to leave, but once she'd settled down she was quite happy to let him go. This was good for my parents, as they could have a few days to relax and catch up with the everyday things that needed doing.

I was finding it difficult to handle it all. I would sometimes feel as if I wasn't getting the attention that I deserved and I would become isolated. I'd sometimes just sit in my bedroom for days on end, reading about famous battles like the Somme or Gallipoli. I wanted to ask Dad to tell me some more about his Granddad, but he was always too busy or too tired. The only thing I did learn was that my Great Granddad was called Bill Farrell and that he served in Sheffield's "Pals battalion." Dad had some other photographs of Bill, showing him in a deckchair in a garden, next to Grandma and some other people. Beneath his blazer, he was wearing a shirt and tie and, although the photograph was hazy, I'm certain that the tie was the same tie that George had been wearing. It is difficult to tell anything about a person's character, from such a small photograph, but I began to see Bill as a man with a dry sense of humour, beneath an outwardly serious exterior. Grandma was looking like he'd just said something amusing out of the corner of his mouth, causing her to laugh, but he had kept a straight face, despite being responsible for her obvious amusement.

My sense of isolation eventually led to me having a fight with Amanda, which I caused by deliberately turning the volume too high on the television. She became upset and soon it all spiralled out of control and dad had to separate us. I'd say we were *existing* as a family, rather than actually functioning in any real sense. The worse it got, the more I began to retreat into my own world, which involved reading and absorbing the details of acts of bravery on both sides of World War One. I was frustrated because the one person I knew who was actually *there*, was Mr Spears and the chance to talk to him seemed to have passed me by.

Chapter Four

I was part of a group of children, who started rehearsals for the school Christmas events in November and, as usual, Miss Tuke had been given the responsibility of planning and organising it all. She'd decided that, as a special treat for the residents, we would be performing our show in The Ferns. When I heard her mention it, I immediately started to pay attention to what she was saying because I might get another chance to talk to Mr Spears. I learned that our performance would involve the usual nativity scene with a few carols, which the old people could join in. We would then give out some Christmas gifts and cards, because we knew that many of the Ferns residents did not have any family and we wanted to make it a happy time for them. The whole thing would then be repeated in the school hall, later in the day, for parents to attend.

After many rehearsals, it was time to visit The Ferns, and as Miss Tuke introduced the first carol I could see Mr Spears was sitting behind an old lady who had fallen asleep as soon as the concert had started.

The evening went smoothly and I can remember how happy everyone seemed to be. I'm not a religious person, but Christmas music has the power to bring happiness and optimism like nothing else can do. After the singing, each student was allowed ten minutes to share a Christmas cracker and a mince pie with one of the residents and I made straight for Mr Spears. I took a deep breath and started with, 'Hello, Mr Spears. My name is Matthew, do you remember coming to our concert about World War One?'

He turned to face me, saying, 'Of course I do. I still think about it sometimes. It was a good little show and you were the soldier returning home, weren't you?'

'Yes, that's right. Was it really like that for you?'

'The joining up bit was fun. Larking around with other young lads and training up on the moors. We thought that it'd just be like a free holiday in France and that we'd be home in a few weeks.'

'I found out that My Great-Granddad was in the Sheffield battalion.'

Almost as soon as I had finished this sentence, Mr Spears sat up straight and seemed almost like he was standing to attention on parade.

'He was one of us?'

'I just know from my dad, that he volunteered to join up and that not many of them came home.'

'Someone had the idea of encouraging young men from the same area to join up together and these became known as Pals battalions. I knew nearly all of the Sheffield lads and I had some cousins in the Barnsley lot. What was his name?'

'Bill Farrell.'

Mr Spears hand suddenly gripped the armrest of his wheelchair as he turned to face me.

'Bill? He was your…' The rest of the question died in his mouth.

'Did you know him?'

Mr Spears rolled his wheelchair back a metre or two and stared at me, for what seemed like a minute, but in reality must have only been a few seconds. When he spoke, his voice was fragile and barely above a whisper, 'Bill. It's you! You're back after all these years. How are you? How's Annie? Is she still working for old man Truswell on the farm? My word, you're looking well.'

Faced with this sudden change in Mr Spears, I tried to speak, but it seemed as if he was really seeing me as if I was Bill. We ended up gazing at each other, Mr Spears with a delighted smile on his face and me feeling puzzled and slightly worried. The scene ended, with someone tapping me on the shoulder and asking me to join the other kids at the door, from where we would be taken back to school. I took a last look at the old man and waved. He smiled and waved back, adding, 'Nice to see you again Bill. Call again soon. We've got a lot of catching up to do, and don't forget to give my love to Annie.'

Chapter Five

Though Dad was largely a serious-minded man, I'd forgotten how much fun he could sometimes be. I remember walking past my parents' bedroom and I could see mum sitting up in bed, laughing, as he was sitting in the bedside chair, playing the ukulele and doing his George Formby impressions:

Tee hee! Here's one for Margaret Jennifer Farrell, of Spall Avenue, Sheffield. Poor Margaret's been feeling a bit rough lately, so I hope this'll cheer her up a bit,

Now I go cleanin' windows to earn an honest bob

For a nosy parker it's an interestin' job…'

Decades have since come and gone, but I can't remember hearing mum laughing with any more freedom than she did that day. Eventually, she stopped laughing and said to dad, 'Pete. What time are you going to pick Amanda up?'

'I'll probably set off about half-past one. Do you want to come?'

'No. I need to sort her clothes out for when we go away tomorrow… Pete…'

'Yes?'

'Are you sure she'll be OK on a caravan site? I mean, do you think she'll like it and that we will be able to stay the whole week?'

Dad tried to reassure her, 'Megs darling, we've discussed this several times. Yes, I'm sure it'll be OK. We've done it before. Do you remember that holiday we had in Devon, when she wanted to bring that kid goat home with us and the farmer thought she was stealing it?'

Mum laughed, but there was a hint of sadness in her laughter, 'That seems so long ago. She was more manageable in those days. I'm a bit worried that she won't settle… Life seemed easier then.'

Dad leaned over and kissed her, gently brushing her hair to one side.

'Stop worrying pet! Doctor Byrom advised us to try and get out more often together as a family, and to keep an eye on Matt so he doesn't feel isolated and neglected. He needs a break at half-term.'

Chapter Six

As was the tradition in our family, we'd got halfway to the caravan park, when mum realised that she'd left the front door open and so we turned back home again. Fortunately, we weren't going far, because we'd booked to stay at a caravan site, some twenty miles away, near Matlock. It was mid-afternoon when dad's old car eventually rattled through the gates and on to the field. Amanda had been singing and telling jokes most of the way there, but had now fallen asleep.

While my parents woke Amanda and started unloading our things into the caravan, I was immediately out of the car and exploring what this place had to offer. The site itself was pleasant enough, with swings and a games building, in which there were fruit machines and a table-tennis table. There was also a pond with swans and ducks, and I made a mental note to go and throw them some bread after tea. Best of all, the site was next to a cricket field, which held the promise that there might be a match played over the weekend for me to watch. I loved cricket and showed some promise as a cricketer. My ambition was to get into the secondary school cricket team and be spotted by a Yorkshire scout, before being invited to wear the white rose of Yorkshire and to eventually play for England. I made a note to myself to climb over the fence in the morning and have a close look inside the pavilion.

After we had eaten, Dad thought that it would be an excellent idea if we went on a family walk across the Derbyshire countryside and breathed in some "good old fashioned fresh air." We ambled through a number of pretty villages, each with stone-built cottages and its own distinctive character. Dad was in his element and, behind him, Mum and Amanda walked hand in hand, picking wild flowers and enjoying the individual scents. I was at the back, thinking about cricket and the possibility of perhaps meeting some other kids on the caravan site and playing games of cricket until the last possible minute, before bed-time.

I remember thinking that I'd seen my fair share of narrow lanes and small churches, when I noticed an elegant war memorial, located proudly in the centre of a village square. It was a tall stone pillar, with a cross at the top and a plaque at its foot, with a list of names and this message:

I had read it several times before I became aware of a hand in mine, and Amanda was standing next to me. She was wearing her favourite cream, flower-patterned dress and sandals, with a daisy chain necklace draped around her neck. I remember noticing how pretty she was and that she had our mum's delicate features and rich, copper-coloured hair.

'Hello, Bill? What are you thinking about?'

'I'm Matt, not Bill, and, if you must know, I was thinking about how many people from around here died in the war.'

'I think it's funny really.'

'What's funny about it? I don't understand what you mean.'

'I mean that they call it the *Great War* and it wasn't really that great at all was it? Not for these men.'

'You're right Amanda, but I think the word great must mean that it was a massive war and not *great*, if you know what I mean.'

'I suppose so. Anyway, it's very sad isn't it? Do you ever wish you'd actually been there?'

'I sometimes imagine what it must have been like, but I wouldn't have wanted to be in the trenches, with all that mud and rats... but...'

'But what?'

'Well, I'd love to have met our Great-Granddad and found out what he was like and what did in the war.'

'I think you'll meet him and find all this out one day. I know, I'll arrange for you to meet him. Is that OK? Come on Bill; look how far ahead mum and dad are. I'll race you!'

She let go of my hand and we hurried towards the distant figures of our parents.

Chapter Seven

The next three days were as enjoyable as any that we'd ever had. I watched a cricket match and even got to look around the pavilion at some of the photographs of past teams and trophies that the club had won over previous decades. One of the players noticed me bowling and asked if I wanted to come and play for their junior team, which thrilled me beyond words.

Mum seemed much more relaxed than I'd seen her for quite some time and Dad spent a lot of time talking and walking with Amanda.

That all changed at about five-thirty on the Wednesday morning when I was awoken by the sound of Mum's screams. Amanda was missing. Her bed was empty and the caravan door was open. Dad raced across to the toilet block, only to find it empty. I got out of bed and with a torch helped my parents to search the all of the unlit spaces between the caravans and around the caravan site, but there was no sign of her. Very soon, several people from other caravans appeared and joined in, but as dawn approached she remained missing. The police arrived and started to organise a search across the nearby countryside.

Eventually, I heard a shout from somewhere over to my left.

'She's here, in the pond. Somebody help me get her out. Quickly please. Over here!'

When I reached the edge of the pond, Amanda was lying pale and lifeless, surrounded by weeds, with her eyes partially open. Dad had put her in the recovery position and was surrounded by worried looking people as he emptied her mouth of mud and, before setting about the task of trying to revive her. He breathed into her mouth and massaged her heart, while constantly asking Amanda to stay with us. After what seemed like an hour, there was a retching sound and Amanda coughed up some more muddy water. She was alive, but unconscious.

Such was the shock of it all, that I can remember only parts of that day. Dad's twin sister, Auntie Jenny, came to pick me up and take me back to her house, while mum and dad went in the ambulance with Amanda. Jenny's family did their best to entertain me and provide some distraction from the reality that Amanda may die at any time, but I could not focus on anything else. More than once, I burst into tears.

Dad turned up the next afternoon and we set off back to our house. On the way, I asked, 'How's Amanda, Dad?'

Dad pulled the car over and said, 'Matt. I really can't lie to you. Amanda is in a coma: meaning that she's alive but deeply unconscious. When we got her out of the water, it looks like she was actually dead, but somehow, she was able to come back. Her brain was starved of oxygen and the doctors don't know if she'll ever wake up and, if she does, what shape she'll be in.'

I tried to think of some questions to ask him, but I couldn't, so we drove the rest of the way home in silence.

Chapter Eight

The final half-term in primary school should have been one of nervous anticipation at the prospect of going up to Saint Aiden's Academy across town, but Amanda's condition over-shadowed everything. One of my parents was with her day and night and I have clear memories of hearing Mum crying and hearing snatches of conversation between my parents, which involved phrases like "no change" or "same as usual."

Eventually, it was time to leave school and start the long summer holiday, but while other kids had the prospect of endless fun ahead of them, my family were hunkered under the cloud of Amanda's permanent sleep and the seemingly futile hopes that she would ever come home.

Sometime during the second week of the holiday, Jenny called to see how we were doing. She had married Uncle Martin when she was still a teenager and Martin's career in the army had resulted in them spending years living abroad. Jenny and Martin's kids were a little older than Amanda and me, and as a result we'd had very little in common and only saw them on family occasions.

Jenny had had an idea, 'Megs, I've had an idea about giving Matt a bit of a break from all this worry about poor Amanda.'

Mum had been worrying about me and so was instantly interested in anything that might cheer me up, 'I'll listen to any idea about how to help him. What is it?'

What came next was about the best thing that anyone could have had. Jenny suggested that her son Andrew and I could go camping in the area where our great granddad had been, during the war. Andrew had been there before and knew one or two places to stay. He was in the army and did not have to be back at Catterick for a couple of weeks and would be more than happy to take me away for a short break. Jenny gave Mum plenty of assurances that my cousin would look after me and that we'd eat proper food and not go in any pubs.

It was agreed that Andrew would pick me up at eight-thirty on the following Monday morning. We'd drive to Dover and get a ferry over to France and I'd get to see the battlefields for myself.

Later that evening, as I was watching TV and imagining what I might see on my expedition, dad came over and sat next to me.

'Son,' he said. 'I want to talk to you about Amanda.'

'What about her? Is something wrong?'

'Not exactly, but you see, Matty, that's sort of the problem. Nothing has changed at all and Amanda isn't showing any signs of getting better or regaining consciousness and Mum and I are worried that...'

'Tell me.'

'The thing is that we don't know how long she'll be like this and a time might come when the doctors might decide that she'll never wake up and that we should stop helping her breathe. Meaning that she'll die.'

'They can't do that can they?'

'No, not without a lot of thought obviously, and your mum and I would have to agree. We're just very worried about the future that's all. I'd like you to go and see her before you go away.'

'OK Dad. When?'

'We'll go tomorrow I think. Yes, tomorrow. Right, off to bed, Matt.'

Chapter Nine

In 1973, the Children's Hospital looked much the same as it does today. It is an imposing Victorian brick building, located across from a park, on a hill just outside the city centre. Dad parked on the road outside the hospital and we made our way to Amanda's room, where mum had been "on duty" since earlier in the morning. The room had a spectacular view across the city and to the east; I could see the steel works, belching brown smoke over Attercliffe.

Amanda had a tube in her mouth, through which a machine was pumping air into her lungs, making a noise rather like a dragon snoring in its sleep. At her bedside were many of her favourite soft toys, together with some magazines and books about the Beatles. Her face was deathly pale and her auburn hair, now shoulder length, fell loosely across her pillow.

As mum saw us arrive, she said to Amanda, 'Hey look! Dad and Matty are here to see you. That's nice isn't it?'

Dad took his cue, adding, 'Hello my little one. Say "hello" to your brother.'

We all took turns to talk to her and as I held her hand, I remembered our conversation by the war memorial.

'Hey Amanda! I'm going to France next week, with Andrew. We're going to see where Bill and his friends went in 1914.'

I thought that it must have been my imagination and that I felt the faintest movement of Amanda's hand in mine. I continued, 'I'll bring you something back and when you're better, we can go together.'

There was another slight movement of her little finger. I told my parents and they also held her hand and told her about what we could do as a family when this was over, but there were no more signs of movement. On the way home, Dad suggested that perhaps it was just wishful thinking that had made me want to believe that Amanda had responded to what I'd said. Mum told him off for being tactless and they had an argument about it. The disagreement eventually ended and, after he'd taken us home, Dad went back to spend another night at Amanda's bedside.

Chapter Ten

As the day of departure approached, mum became increasingly anxious about whether it was a good idea to let me go camping with Andrew, who she hadn't seen in years and who was still only twenty-two. Jenny re-assured mum that Andrew would look after me and that we'd have a good time; after all, we were only going to be away for a short time and Andrew was an experienced driver on European roads. The plan was to start in Ypres and see the Menin Gate, before driving south and visiting the area around the Somme. Eventually, mum's worries eased a little and, on Monday morning, after a few sloppy kisses from her and a firm handshake from Dad, I climbed in Andrew's car and we were on our way.

Before he started the engine, Andrew shook my hand and said how nice it was to see me again. As we headed south towards Dover, I learned that Andrew shared my interests in both sport and military history. Equally pleasingly, he had brought along some maps and library books as well as several bags of sweets for us to share on the way, so, as we got to know one another, we talked about the war and ploughed our way through seemingly endless quantities of cola cubes and sherbet lemons.

'What do you actually *do* in the army?' I asked.

'Good question. Well, I'm in the Royal Engineers. We do everything that needs to be done as well as fighting. For example, if we were in a battle, we'd build bridges over rivers or we might blow them up if needed. At other times, we'll clear minefields or build camps. In fact, we're the people they all go to when they want things done in a hurry.'

'So, why did you join the army?'

'That's another good question. I wasn't that brilliant at school work, but I still wanted to learn new skills and to see the world outside military bases. Dad suggested that I apply and, as soon as I walked through the door of the recruitment office, I knew that it was what I wanted to do. It's tough work and we're away from home a lot of the time, but when you're part of a tight unit, then it's like a family and I like that.'

'Can you play sports in the army?'

'Of course! When we're given time off, a lot of the boys do stuff like football or cricket. It's important to remain fit and physical training is part of the daily routine. Do you play any sport, Matthew?'

This was my chance to tell him about my ambitions to play cricket for a good team and then for England.

Andrew replied, 'Did you know that our great granddad played cricket and football in his younger days? I'm sure that someone once told me that he had the chance to play professional football and cricket, but that the pay wasn't good enough to support a family, so he didn't take up the offer. When I was a really little kid and we were in the country, we used to stay with him and I vaguely remember playing cricket with him on his back garden. He was really old, but he could still play all the strokes.'

The knowledge that Andrew had spent some time with Bill, prompted a stream of other questions from me and, from out of the mists of time, some of Bill's life began to take shape.

I learned that Bill had worked for a company called Gibbs Brothers and that he died suddenly. In his final years, Bill had visited the area where we were going, in order to visit the war graves and to pay his respects to his brother and his many fallen comrades. Andrew remembered him as being a quiet and thoughtful man who would spend hours over a crossword in the local paper and who liked to eat honey on fresh bread.

'Andrew, did he ever mention being in the war?'

'I don't think I ever heard him talk about it, or being in the Home Guard in World War Two.'

It turns out that in the Second World War Bill had joined the Home Guard and trained up on the moors at Redmires. I thought about how he must have felt, when his son and daughter-in-law were killed in the road traffic accident and, how he and Grandma stepped up from being grandparents, to once again being responsible for bringing up children. After an hour without speaking, another question came into my mind, 'Andrew? What about Great Grandma? Do you remember much about her?'

'Nothing at all. I know that she was unwell for a couple of years and I can remember my mum telling me how she'd being diagnosed with cancer and that she was in hospital for a long time. That reminds me, I meant to ask you about Amanda, how is she?'

Andrew listened as I recounted the incident in the pond, before saying, 'I think she's a survivor: just like Bill.'

Chapter Eleven

The ferry pitched and rolled over the tumbling waves of the English Channel and we arrived in Calais feeling seasick but relieved to be back on solid ground. Andrew was keen to get out of the port and across northern France to our camp site, without any further delay. It was the early hours of the morning, before we reached the village of Kaai, where we were staying and, rather than struggle to put up our tents in the dark, we decided to sleep in the car.

We awoke to a warm and sunny Belgian morning, which enabled us to pitch our tent, eat some breakfast and explore the amenities of the site, which were basic but adequate. The toilets and washrooms were small but reasonably clean and everyone seemed welcoming. We had to queue up to use the shower, but both felt much better afterwards and were now ready to catch the bus into Ypres.

From a tourist information leaflet in English I learned that much of Ypres had been destroyed or damaged in the war and that Germany had been forced to pay for the repair of much of the town centre. The first place that took away my breath was the Cloth Hall. It's a huge building that looks medieval but is in fact only a copy of the original that was destroyed by artillery fire and it is now the home of the Flanders Fields Museum. We could hear the bell ringing in the tower from across town and I remember standing outside; a small boy in a large crowd of visitors, everyone seemingly gazing up in awe at the beauty of the place and sharing the excitement of being there. Inside, the museum had displays of just about everything that I could have wanted to see, including guns, boots and uniforms from both sides of the battles. The gas masks, in particular, caught my imagination, and I remember sensing what horrors must have been experienced by Bill and so many other young men as they lurched forward through a hail of bullets, into a yellow cloud of death. A helpful guide explained some of the physical damage that came with trench warfare and how foot-rot could quickly set in and cause a soldier to have his foot amputated.

Over the course of the day we must have visited every museum, stopping only to eat a plate of chips in a small cafe on a side street. I bought a postcard with a colour photograph of Saint Martin's Cathedral and some Belgian chocolate for Amanda. At around five o'clock, as we crossed the main square, Andrew shouted, 'Look! That bus is taking people out to the Menin Gate. Quick, let's get on!'

Before I could ask any questions, we were on a cramped, little bus, heading out of town. Fortunately, the journey was not a long one, and within no more than ten minutes we were there.

The "Gate" which is in fact a huge ornately carved stone archway, commemorates the thousands of Commonwealth soldiers who were killed in this area before August 1917 and who have no grave. I tried to count the names on the memorial, but there are too many to take in. As if this was not overwhelming enough, we learned that the soldiers who died *after* August 1917 are remembered at an equally huge memorial elsewhere.

For a half an hour I circled the Menin Gate, open-mouthed, trying to process what I was experiencing, until I became aware that all of the background noise and chatter had died down and had had been replaced by stillness and silence. I heard someone whisper, 'It's starting Eric, Listen!'

From beneath the arch, a bugler began to play the Last Post and I began to understand how that short piece of music can reduce the most hard-hearted person to tears. I noticed that, standing next to me, an elderly man, wearing some war medals on his jacket, was sobbing quietly to himself as the bugler reached the final notes. I imagined that he was here to pay his respects to fallen friends. I thought of George Spears and how much he would have liked to be here.

Eventually, the crowd of visitors melted sombrely away and we caught the last bus back to Ypres. As we walked back along the quiet country lanes, towards the campsite, I asked, 'What are we going to do tomorrow?'

'I'm not sure. I haven't thought about it yet. Have you any ideas?'

I said that I was tired and that I might just hang around the campsite tomorrow and possibly go for a walk in the woods and fields.

'Good idea, let's take it easy for a while,' Andrew said, 'and after all, most of these fields were where battles took place. It's really hard to believe, when it all looks so peaceful now.'

'Do you mean fields like that one?' I said, pointing across the countryside.

'Yes. As you can see it's just farmland, but there might still be unexploded shells lying around.'

'Honestly?'

'God's truth, Matt. I would also imagine that these fields are full of ghosts and spirits. I wouldn't want to be out there in the dark. Oh no!'

After breakfast, we both felt at we had sufficient energy to explore some more military history and therefore decided to spend the day by visiting one of the notable sites of the Second World War. It was here that so many American soldiers were lost in the particularly brutal winter of 1944-1945. I had that same feeling as I'd had around the farmland near the campsite. I sensed that while nature had now reclaimed the area, there was the same eerie silence and sense of super-natural sadness lingering in the air.

What I wanted now, was to get back on the trail of Bill's war, so Andrew said that we would go to visit a place where that we knew Bill had been. It was time to see Serre-les-Puisieux.

It took several hours to get there and we frequently found ourselves lost in the seemingly endless and beautiful French countryside. Once or twice we tried to get directions from local people, but no one spoke English and so we wandered through a maze of country lanes, becoming ever more frustrated with every dead-end. Eventually, on the D919, there was a road sign for the village of Puisieux and we could start to relax.

Having paid a farmer rather more than enough to camp in his field, we explored Puisieux and found that it had only one main road, with houses and barns on either side. At a crossroads, there was a cream-coloured, stone war memorial with several hundred names carved on a plinth at its base. After buying some provisions from a local shop, it was time go back and settle down for the night.

Chapter Twelve

We'd seen some other tents in the field when we arrived, but hadn't taken much notice of them and it wasn't until the morning that we had a chance to see the other people camping around us. Most of the other visitors seemed to be young people, back-packing around Europe, intent on having a good time. Once we'd eaten breakfast, I noticed that Andrew had taken a liking to a girl that he'd met in the queue for the washroom and I thought that he might appreciate some time to talk to her without having to worry about me, so I decided to go and find the Sheffield Memorial Park. There seemed no harm in going alone, after all I'd pored over so many maps and read enough library books to know exactly where I needed to go.

Once outside the campsite, I turned right and walked for around a quarter of a mile along a steep, rutted track, with a tall hedgerow on either side. About half way up I noticed something metallic, glinting in the long grass. Instinctively, I stopped to see what it was and there at my feet was a shell case. It had a few scratches and marks on it and the lettering on the side was now difficult to read, but it had to have been from the battle. As I held it, I put my nose inside and imagined that I could still smell the explosive. I couldn't wait to show it to Andrew.

I reached the crest of the slope and went down a track. My pace quickened as I approached what was unmistakably the main gate of the memorial, where I stopped to read the plaques that had been dedicated to the fallen of Sheffield and other northern towns. I realised that I was standing in what had been the epicentre of the battle itself.

Across the road was the cemetery, and the now familiar ranks of the fallen. As I ambled along each line of head stones, I read some of their names. Among them were: P Long, A Longley and A D McKenzie, all aged under twenty five and all killed on July the first 1916. The grave of Bill's older brother, Joe, was at the end of a row and this was as close to Bill as I had ever been. Bill must have stood on this spot and read the carved epitaph:

58396
Private
J.P. Farrell
Sheffield City Battalion
Y&L Regiment
1/7/16.
Age 24.

Standing there alone, I was sure that I could hear the sound of male voices. Not one, but perhaps hundreds of men talking at once, and they were growing louder with every passing moment. I tried to focus on one voice and listen to what it was saying, but I could only hear fragmented parts of a conversation between the owner of the voice and someone else. The voice told me that he wanted to go home and he wanted to see Annie again.

Chapter Thirteen

You've come a long way to find me Matthew and it's only fair that I should tell you my story; after all it's your history as well. We may be generations apart, but we're family and we're shaped by many of the same forces. Just remember that a lot has changed since I was your age and the world you live in is a very different place to mine and it's changing fast. Please don't think of me as any sort of hero. I did what I thought was right at the time and I paid a heavy price for it, though not the ultimate price that was paid by Our Joe and many of my friends. If at any point, you want me to stop, then I will and you can go back to your life and forget about it all, but I have to warn you that if you decide to follow me into battle, you will not be spared the horrors of that day in 1916. The places and people that I describe will appear as real to you as the world that you live in. Think of it as if you are me and you'll understand where you come from. I sense that you are eager to come along, so let's get started.

***

In 1914, we were living at 32, Carlton Road in Attercliffe. I shared a mid-terraced house with Mother, Dad and my older brother, Joe. When he was young, someone once started to call him 'Our Joe' and the name just stuck. Attercliffe is very different now, but we lived on the eastern side of the city, among the dozens of foundries and factories. Future generations will know that it was from places like Attercliffe, that the nation was built. The Manchester, Sheffield and Lincolnshire railway line was just over the road from us and as a boy I'd stand on the bridge and look down in wonder on the steam engines as they roared beneath me, throwing up a storm of steam and sparks. On a still day, the Attercliffe air was often dense with smoke and fumes and life for us working people in Sheffield was tough and often short. Dad was a labourer in the nearby coke ovens and, despite having an injured back, he never missed a day's work. Mother stayed at home, keeping the house presentable and doing endless amounts of washing.

She was the heart of our family and the person who we all relied upon to keep everything together. Things simply didn't get done without her. We were about as normal as you could have found anywhere and, as was often the case, just about everyone within a mile of our house knew everyone else's business. If you look at a Lowry painting, you'll see us in there somewhere.

The Parker's house was back to back with ours, separated only by the narrow alleyway between the rows of terraces. The Parkers had twin girls, born in the same year as I was, but that's about all the two sisters had in common. Ruby was a lively girl and always happy to join in with the boys in games of street football. She was as strong as any lad and was often the one most caked in mud and blood after a match. Annie, on the other hand, preferred the company of animals and used to help out at Thompson's stables, mucking out and feeding the horses. I paid very little attention to her, preferring Ruby's energy and lively company.

The accident in the steelworks that claimed the life of Ruby and Annie's dad shocked the whole community and, without his income, her mother soon found herself with no option, other than to leave the area and move in with their grandmother, who lived two miles away in Darnall. That was two years before and, while I had occasionally found myself walking through the area where they live, I had not seen any of the Parker family since then. Industrial accidents weren't unusual; most of us in Attercliffe knew someone who had lost a friend or family member in that way, besides which, in the spring of 1914, there were darker clouds on the horizon, although it would be several months before young men of the city answered a call to arms.

After leaving school, I'd started at Gibbs Brothers cutlery works and by the age of eighteen I fancied that I knew everything about the world of work. Our Joe had been there a couple of years and he recommended me to the management, and that's how I ended up working alongside him. There must have been twenty young blokes at our place and, though we worked hard, we had our share of fun and tomfoolery when the boss was away. It's fair to say that we were all mates and we'd always happily cover for each other in an emergency. That's how I avoided getting into trouble for being late for work.

One morning, I'd been waiting for a tram into Sheffield when I saw a young woman, waiting for a tram on the other side of the road.

She had the prettiest face and most perfect figure that I'd ever seen and, despite being in working clothes, she somehow looked more elegant and stylish than anyone else around her. I was transfixed by her and, though I tried not to be obviously staring at her, subtlety was never my strong point. She sensed this and turned away to begin a conversation with someone next to her in the queue. Eventually, I went towards the city centre on one tram and she went out towards the outskirts of the city on another. That is until the following morning, when we were both back at our usual places and the charade was played out once more.

I was totally captivated by her and, about a week later, I found the courage to cross the road and stand in her queue. I didn't care where I'd end up, just as long as I might have the chance to talk to her. After we'd climbed onto the tram, I was able to push someone aside and get the seat next to her and that's when I realised that she was Annie Parker. She'd blossomed from an awkward, callow girl into this beautiful young woman. She had dark wavy hair and hazel eyes, like no others that I'd ever seen before. I introduced myself and we began talking. She remembered me and asked about everyone in my family. She told me that Ruby was now married with a baby girl and that she herself now worked at Truswell's farm out at Loxley.

'And you go all that way, every day?' I asked.

'I don't really mind,' she explained. 'I love animals and I get to spend plenty of time with the horses, so that suits me. Mrs Truswell lets me take home any spare eggs and off-cuts of meat, so it has its advantages. Anyway, I'll be moving in soon, so I won't have to travel. Where are you going today, don't you usually go towards town?'

I briefly tried to think of an excuse for going in the wrong direction, but I could only come up with, 'I work in Sharrow but I thought I'd go this way for a change.'

She looked puzzled and asked if I often went in the opposite direction to the one I actually needed. I had no way out of this and, realising that we would soon be arriving at her stop, I took my chance and asked if we could meet and perhaps go somewhere for a walk. She said that she would think about it and that if I asked her tomorrow, then she'd let me know. She got off at the top of Loxley Hill; and so began an anxious wait until the following morning.

Sleep was impossible. I went through every possible scenario. She might say "no," and then what would I do? She might already have a boyfriend, and I imagined some bloke at the farm, taking a fancy to her and asking her out. If I'd worked there, then I would have.

The next morning I got out of bed a few minutes earlier, as I wanted to take a careful shave and look at my absolute best. Our Joe watched me preening myself in the mirror and couldn't resist saying, 'William Farrell. Why are you tarting yourself up so much today? Do you, by any chance, happen to be smitten by a girl?'

Typically of Joe, he'd worked it out straight away and over breakfast, I told him about meeting Annie.

'Well, strike while the iron is hot, because I happen to know that other blokes are keen on her as well as you.'

Pretending to be nonchalant, I asked who, and he replied, 'George Spears for one.'

George Spears? *The* George Spears from work? Are you serious?'

'The very same. I heard that he's already asked her out and that she's keeping him waiting as well.'

That was all the motivation I needed and I was soon waiting for Annie to arrive at her usual morning spot. I could have caught an earlier tram, but I held back and waited for it to fill up and leave. Eventually, Annie came around the corner and took her place in the queue. After a few minutes, she looked over at me and with a nervous gulp of air I crossed over and said, 'Have you decided?'

With a hint of a smile, she looked me up and down before replying, 'Yes. I've decided that I trust you enough, to accompany me somewhere. Have you any ideas Mr Farrell?'

Trying to contain my happiness, I suggested that I could meet her at the main gate of High Hazels Park at midday on Sunday. We might then go on a walk around the park, before having a picnic. She seemed happy with this idea and agreed to be at the park gates.

'That'll upset George Spears,' I thought.

Chapter Fourteen

Despite working next to George for most of the week, I decided to say nothing to him about my arrangement to meet Annie on Sunday. He clearly had no idea about it and in any case, rather than courting girls, he was usually much more interested in anything vaguely football related. I lost count of the times that he repeated his prediction that this was definitely Wednesday's year and that they would win the Cup.

George was a more than decent amateur footballer himself and, had apparently had been watched by talent scouts from a number of clubs. He was tall, with a mop of unruly dark hair, and had an eye for goal; in fact his goal-scoring feats were frequently mentioned in the local paper.

My thoughts on Saturday morning were focused on playing well for the local cricket team. I was a real sportsman in those days and I'd been having an excellent season, scoring lots of runs. We were playing at our home ground, down on Staniforth Road. The opposition were a team from Heeley and the game went totally our way from the start. They were out cheaply and, even after a very leisurely tea break, Tom Kennedy and I were able to score all the runs needed for victory without anyone else having to bat. The game was over by four thirty, which everyone believed to be some kind of record. As I was relaxing in the pavilion after the game, someone said that a bloke was waiting outside and that he wanted to talk to me. I asked him if he knew who it was, but he didn't, so I made my way to see for myself. I instantly recognised the visitor as Harry Martin, from Chapelfield CC, one of the better cricket clubs in the city. We'd known each other since school and had often crossed swords on both cricket and football fields. His team were always a little better than ours and had beaten us more often than not. They had lovely ground over in Ecclesfield and played in the division above us. Over recent seasons some of their players had gone on to play for Yorkshire. Short, stocky and always to the point, Harry raised himself to his full height of five foot two and said, 'Afternoon Bill. I've been sent by our committee to come and ask you if you want to play for us next year. We're after winning the league next season and we reckon 1915 is going to be our year. Nothing can stop us and we think that you're just the bloke we need at the top of the batting order.'

I told him that I would think about it and let him know by the end of the season. We shook hands and Harry seemed happy with the fact that I was prepared to at least think about it.

I walked home with a head spinning with the thought of both playing cricket for Chapelfield in 1915 and, if things went well tomorrow, possibly courting Annie on a long-term basis. I was on my way.

Dad was in the back yard, when I arrived home and I told him what had happened. He was all in favour of me joining Chapelfield, and said, 'If it were me, I'd take the chance and play for them. They're a bit of a big-headed lot up there, but you'll be fine. You're definitely good enough and I've always told you to push yourself and see how far you can go.'

From up a ladder, where he was replacing a roof tile on the outside toilet, Our Joe said, 'Dad's right Bill. What have you got to lose? A club like that wouldn't ask, if they didn't think you were up to it. Give me a minute and I'll be finished up here, then there's something I was going to ask you as well.'

I said that it sounded interesting and that I'd put the kettle on.

As it happens, Mother was already making a cup of tea for everyone and so ten minutes later as we drank it, Our Joe told me what was on his mind.

'Look Bill, let's hope that it doesn't happen, but I was listening to some blokes in the pub last night and they were talking about the possibility of war. I didn't understand all of what they were saying, but the idea was that there might be a war in Europe before long. Anyway, I got to thinking that if that should happen, then I'm willing to do my bit and go and fight.'

I was shaken, but managed to answer, 'Some of the boys at work have been talking about it, but surely it's just talk and that's all there is to it.'

'Yes, it might all be rubbish, but what I'm saying is that blokes like us have got to be prepared to do our bit and if they needed us and a lot of us joined up together, we might not even need to fight at all. Just think about it for a minute, when are we ever likely to have the chance to see the world? Would you be prepared to join up with me?'

It was obvious that Our Joe thought about this a great deal.

Mother and Dad had very different opinions. Dad was of the same mind as Joe and agreed that the chance of anyone actually firing a gun was so small as to not be worth worrying about, but if called upon, then we should be prepared to fight.

'It might do them good to put on a uniform, Jessie. There's never anything wrong with serving the country in her time of need. She gives us what we need and all Englishmen should be prepared to protect the Empire when called upon.'

Mother was horrified by this and seemed close to tears. 'No. I'm not having this talk in my kitchen. You should know better than to be encouraging our sons to risk life and limb fighting. Get out of my sight and I don't want to hear that kind of talk again!'

Dad and Our Joe left the kitchen and I found myself alone with Mother, who, despite trying to look busy washing teacups in the sink, was trying not to cry. I put my arms around her and said, 'Don't worry mother, we'll be fine, we're not daft. Joe will probably forget all about it. You know what he's like.'

I felt Mother shiver as she looked away.

'I hate the thought of you two boys going to war. You're my lads. I've always tried to keep you safe.'

'I know you have,' I said, 'and we wouldn't ever want to upset you, but if the country needed us, then we'd have to do our duty.'

Mother turned to face me and smiled, saying, 'What's this I hear about you and Annie Parker?'

This sudden change of topic caught me by surprise, but it was typical of Mother to change the subject mid-conversation, but I went along with it, 'I'm meeting her at High Hazels tomorrow. It's nothing serious or anything. I bumped into her and sort of asked her if she fancied a walk. That's all.'

'I see. Will you need sandwiches?' She had a way of always trying to ensure that I would be fed, wherever I happened to be.

'Sandwiches?'

'I'll tell you what,' she said, 'we've got some cheese left and one or two tomatoes. I'll make you a couple of sandwiches to take with you. That'll keep the wolf from the door.'

'But Mother…'

Chapter Fifteen

Standing in the sunshine, I was gazing dreamily in one direction, when from behind, a voice said, 'Hello Bill!'

'Bloody hell! You nearly gave me a heart attack, Annie Parker!'

'Sorry. I saw you looking down the road and I just couldn't resist the chance to sneak up on you.' Annie was giggling with pleasure at having made me jump.

'It's fine. I'm glad you came.'

'Of course I came. Did you think I wouldn't?'

'Well…. I've heard tales of blokes waiting for days, sometimes weeks and months and the girl never turns up, so the bloke goes off and joins the army in order to forget.'

'That's not me, so you don't have to join up. Right where are we going?' She put her arm through mine and we set off on our walk through the park.

I'm sure that there were many people promenading through High Hazels, but I don't remember noticing any of them. Annie talked about Ruby's baby and how her mum had struggled to keep the family together after the accident. Plans had been made for both girls to go and live with distant family members, but Annie had refused to go and when Ruby married and left home, things became a little easier financially. The job at Truswell's had come at just the right time and had brought in some much needed income. When she moved over there on a full-time basis, she'd miss her mother, but they'd see each other as often as possible.

I tried to tell her about my cricketing exploits, but she showed no interest at all.

'Silly men in white clothes, hitting a ball with a piece of wood!' was her only comment.

We sat on a park bench and I asked her if she wanted a sandwich. She said that she'd also brought some. It seems that both our mothers had only had cheese and tomato available. She nibbled delicately at her sandwiches while mine disappeared in two bites, causing her to suggest that I should be in a zoo. I pretended to have been deeply upset by the comparison of me with a gorilla and offered to leave, but she just laughed and told me to be quiet and wiped some cheese from around my mouth. She took off her hat and the afternoon sunlight glistened in her hair as she took out her hairgrips and shook it free.

'I hate wearing hats. I like to feel the warm sun on my skin and the wind in my hair.'

A few minutes later we started to hear raised voices, coming from the other side of the hedge from where we were sitting. Two voices became three and it soon escalated into what sounded like an angry crowd. Annie thought that we should get away, but I persuaded her to stay with me and listen to what was being said. She moved closer and held my hand. A deep and more refined voice rose above the others and began to speak in an authoritative voice.

'We socialists must fight this to the end. Thousands of young men will be slaughtered like cattle… and for what? I'll tell you why: so that the rich can become fatter and wealthier. That's why. This is about freedom from capitalist oppression. It's time for socialism in this country and for the common man to take control.'

'Absolutely right,' said another.

'Hear! Hear!' came from someone else.

'Absolute rubbish! Why don't you cowards go and live somewhere else? There will be no war in Europe and all you are doing is scaremongering. Ours is the greatest nation on earth and you should be grateful for everything that it's given you.'

The dissenting voice found itself being jeered at and condemned by all of the others, but refused to stop and the debate continued. Annie and I crept up to the hedge and peered over the top, where we saw around ten men gathered around a placard, on which was written:

Socialists against Slaughter
Workers Unite

We watched and listened for around twenty minutes, as the argument continued. The leader of the protest (the owner of the refined voice) was a well dressed man, with an enormous beard and was frequently pointing his finger at a much smaller man, who was pointing back and clearly reluctant to take a backward step in the argument. Then, almost as suddenly as it started, the crowd dispersed and we could hear birds singing again.

Annie had clearly been listening carefully and asked me, 'What do you think Bill? Are you going to go in the army?'

I said that I had no plans to do so and that there was probably not going to be a war, but I was willing to serve King and country if required.

She looked straight at me, 'Please don't Bill. I'd hate to think of you out there somewhere, being shot at. It's awful. I couldn't stand it.'

I held her close to me for the first time and told her over again that it'd be all right and that most likely there would be no war either this year or anytime soon, but deep down, I was far from certain.

The afternoon passed too quickly and we walked and talked, while sharing an ice cream or two or three. Neither of us wanted it to end, but the realisation that it was growing dark brought us back to reality.

After having walked for what seemed like a thousand miles, I said, 'We've both got work tomorrow, haven't we?' and while this was true, I wasn't keen on having to leave her. As we walked back to her house I asked, 'Will you be going out with George Spears?'

There was a long pause before she answered, 'Why would I want to do that, when I've already got you?'

Chapter Sixteen

We met at the park gates just once more before Annie moved over to Loxley. Her only day off was on Sunday, so I used to walk to Loxley to see her. It was at least five miles either way, but I wasn't bothered. I'd worked out a route that took me through Neepsend and Hillsborough, and then along the Loxley Valley, where only fifty years before so many Sheffielders had died in the flood of 1864.

Mrs Truswell would let me come into the farmhouse for a cup of tea, or, if I was lucky, I might get a glass or two of Mr Truswell's home-brewed beer. Annie and I would spend time talking and walking through the meadows. She knew all the bird songs and tried to teach me to recognise some of them, but I was not as good as her. The only one that I could be sure of, was the skylark, twittering madly as it hovered above its nest. Annie knew a lot about birds and she once gently pulled back the branches of a hedge and showed me a nest in which some chicks waited patiently for the adult bird to return with food.

Things changed on one Sunday in mid-July when we were lying next to each other in some long grass, looking up at cotton-wool clouds drifting across an azure sky. Annie was occupied with looking for shapes of different animals in the clouds, when I looked over at her and realised that this was as happy as I'd ever been. Before then, happiness for me was probably found in a game of football or cricket, especially in the after-glow of being a hero for an hour or two after a match, but in an instant, none of that mattered any longer. To my right, Annie was so involved with cloud shapes, that she seemed unaware that I'd slipped a ring over her finger. It was a piece of scrap steel and I'd found it lying around at work and polished up.

'Annie Parker. I love you and I want to marry you.'

Without pausing her cloud watching, she answered, 'I love you as well, William James Farrell and I'd like to marry you too. Look, look there's an elephant. Can you see it?'

'Are you serious? Have you seen the ring?'

She turned to me and said, 'Yes of course I have and I love it. I'm not really worried about rings, you can buy me one when you're able, but this will do. All I want is to be with you.'

So that was that. We now had to plan how and when we'd tell our families. Annie had been to our house several times and my parents had taken an instant liking to her. Dad, especially, had become very fond of her, because she shared his interest in gardening and especially growing vegetables. They'd sometimes spend so long together on his allotment that I'd have to go and fetch them home. Mother began to see Annie as the daughter that she'd never had. She'd fuss and cluck around Annie, like a mother hen. Only Our Joe seemed slightly reserved when she was around. He seemed more interested in the likelihood of war and the possibility of joining the army; and he wanted me to do it as well.

Matters came to a head, after I'd got home from visiting Annie. I was in high spirits, after she'd agreed to marry me and I thought that nothing could bring me down. All I could see was her face and my thoughts were of how we were going to afford to build a life together. We'd agreed to tell both families on the following Sunday. Annie would come home and we'd go to visit her mother together. After that, we'd tell my folks, which I thought would be the easy part.

It was late evening when I walked in. Mother had gone to bed, while dad and Our Joe were in the living room, smoking and chatting.

'Here he is. Lover boy returns home!' Dad joked,

'Stop it Dad,' I replied. 'You were young once and I'm sure you courted mother in some romantic way. Didn't you?'

'I can't remember that long ago. God was a lad that's for sure. Anyway, I'm off up now. See you in the morning, you two.'

Dad went upstairs and Our Joe seized his opportunity.

'Well?'

'Well what?' I answered.

'Are you prepared to fight if needed? They say that it's every man's patriotic duty to fight and that anyone who doesn't is a coward.'

I was becoming annoyed and wanted to avoid any thought of war and of spoiling my dream of being with Annie, 'Who says this?'

Joe didn't seem ready for this question and now flustered, he said, 'Everyone Bill. All the lads say they'll go if needed. The only two who haven't said they'll volunteer are you and George Spears.'

'What has George said?

'He said that he'd think about it, but would rather be a professional footballer.'

I laughed at this and said that it was typical of him to be thinking about football at this time. Joe went back to the matter in hand, 'I want to know what you would do.'

I thought that I had to tell him what had happened earlier, as I might explain things.

'Annie and I are getting married. I asked her today, and she agreed.'

Joe's facial expressions changed about four times in as many seconds, 'What! Are you joking?'

'No, I'm serious. Never been more serious, and that's why I'm not sure about ever joining up, war or no war.'

Joe sat back in his chair and closed his eyes, as if trying to take in what I'd told him. There was silence for a minute or two before he offered his hand, 'Congratulations little brother, I'm right chuffed for you. When are you telling Mother and Dad?'

'Annie's coming over next Sunday and we're doing it then.'

'I'll say nothing, but I mean what I say about fighting for our country if called upon and I'd want you next to me in battle, because we could look after each other and no harm can come to us.'

Chapter Seventeen

Darling Annie,

I hope that you are well, over there in the countryside. How are the horses? I can't wait to see you next Sunday, when we go and give everyone our news. I had a dream that that you changed your mind and so I was going to walk over there after work tonight, just to make sure that you haven't, but I was really tired and so I decided not to. I hope you don't mind.

Our Joe has got this thing in his mind about one day, having to go to war for the country and has been trying to persuade me to join up as well, but of course, I wouldn't do anything like that without talking to you first, though I'm sure that you would be proud of me if I did. Every man has to do what he thinks is right.

Anyway, let's not worry about that, as I'm much more interested in seeing you and hearing your voice again. Are you still wearing the ring? I hope so, because it was very expensive you know!

Dad said that he wishes you were able to lend a hand on the allotment, because his back is hurting a lot recently. It's nice to be needed isn't it?

Anyway, I must go off to bed now, but not before telling you that I love you more than ever.

Sweet dreams my little one.

Your loving Bill.

P.S. I'll meet you outside the Anvil Arms at Ten on Sunday morning. Don't be late!

P.P.S. Don't forget to ask Mr Truswell to let you start work later on Monday, because you'll have to walk back in the morning or get a tram.

Chapter Eighteen

'I could have walked on my own,' Annie said. 'You didn't have to meet me here.'

She knew that I would have gone all the way to Loxley if she'd asked me, and that it was no trouble to wait for her.

'Did you get my letter?' I asked.

'Yes I did and your dream was right. I've decided to marry George Spears instead of you. He's been coming to visit me every night after work and he's bought me a proper engagement ring and not just a piece of scrap of metal from off the floor.' She said all this with a straight face and for a moment I began to believe her. It was only when she looked at me and smiled that I was sure that she wasn't serious.

When we arrived on her street, Annie's mother was standing on her doorstep, waiting for us. I'd known her since I was a kid and she'd always been an energetic and lively woman, but on that day I couldn't help but notice how frail she was for someone who was barely into her fifties. Her hair had turned prematurely white and her face was lined with the anxieties of having become a widow so unexpectedly, with two young children to raise. Annie's grandmother was now unwell and bedridden upstairs, so the strain on Mrs. Parker seemed to be unending.

Later that afternoon, we were sitting in a small parlour sipping tea, with Annie sitting next to her mother on the settee and I wasted no time in asking for her permission to marry Annie. I can't remember what I said, but from somewhere I was able to find the appropriate words, without necessarily putting them in the right order.

Once I'd got that part over, Annie's mother got up and, from a shelf, brought down a photograph of her husband. She looked at it for a while, before saying, 'My Arthur would have liked you. I can tell that you love Annie and I hope you'll make her happy. What I want is for my Annie to have longer with her man than I did with him. I'd give anything to be able to spend just one more day with him, just a day. I wouldn't mind if he was just sitting there, where you are, reading the paper and grumbling about the neighbours, like he used to. He used to say that life's too short to waste on regrets and what might have been and he was right. So, have you made any plans for the wedding?'

'No, we haven't yet, but I'll take care of her, I promise. I'll make Arthur proud of me and I'll take care of his daughter.'

'Do you love him, Annie?'

'Yes, mum.'

'Well, that's all that matters isn't it?' she said.

The conversation soon turned to the practical aspects of where we might get married and if we could ever afford a house. The truth was that we hadn't made any decisions and deep down we both knew that I was likely to be going away soon. Annie would continue to work at Truswell's and there was a small chance of one of the farm worker's cottages becoming vacant, which might allow us to settle there. As things were, we would have to carry on working and wait.

Over at my house, it seems as if Our Joe had not been able to resist telling our Mother and Dad about the engagement, because when we arrived, they were waiting and ready to start a party. Mother had baked a cake and Dad had made a special effort to put on some clean clothes and try to look presentable. There were flowers in vases and a few bottles of beer to open. Mother kissed Annie and Dad shook my hand. When there was a quiet moment, with Annie holding my hand, I said to everyone, 'We were going to tell you all that we're going to get married, but it looks like somebody couldn't keep quiet! Anyway, now you all know.'

Looking back, I'm sure that afternoon was the happiest we'd had as a family. The world might have been sliding towards war, but that little terraced house vibrated with laughter and love. At one point, some of the neighbours turned up and joined in the celebrations and when the pub opened at six o'clock that was the cue for the men to go to the pub and drink more beer.

Dad decided to stay and have 'just one more pint' with some of his workmates, leaving Joe and I to walk home together. Annie wanted to be back at her mother's house by nine and I'd promised to walk her home.

'Well little brother,' he said, 'have you decided what you're doing about the army?'

'I'll come with you, if we have to go.'

'Good man! I'm proud of you. Have you told Annie?'

I said that I'd promised her that she'd be the first to know when I'd made up my mind and, with a shiver of guilt, I realised that was my first broken promise to Annie.

Half an hour later, on the way to her mother's house, I told her what I'd said to Our Joe. I didn't need to wait for an answer.

'I'm not surprised really, because I knew you were going to. Today was supposed to be the happiest day of my life and you go and spoil it by telling me that you'd rather die than be my husband. How could you? I've lost my dad and now I'm going to lose you. Is it me? What have I done?'

'Listen to me Annie, please… '

'Shut up! Go home. Go back to your brother. You listen to him more than you listen to me. I'm just your little woman aren't I? I'm sure when you're with your friends in the army, fighting somewhere, you'll have a big laugh about it – poor Annie, and how she'll be waiting at the door like a little lapdog. Bill… I can't stand the thought of you throwing your life away, when you want to spend it with me. Besides which, what's it all about anyway?

This was the first time I'd seen Annie angry about anything and I understood how she felt, but the urge to do what I thought was the right thing for the country was what had driven me to this decision. To refuse to fight, would have marked me as a coward and someone without pride. I had to do it and I was totally at Annie's mercy as to whether she would forgive me.

'I want you to have this.'

Reaching in my pocket I took out my Grandmother's engagement ring that Mother had given me earlier in the day and slipped it onto Annie's ring finger.

'Annie Parker, no bullet will stop me coming home to you. If I ever go, then when I get home we won't be parted. I'll make sure that you get everything that you'll ever want.'

In the lamplight, I could see her eyes were swollen with tears.

'What you're doing is taking away the only thing I want. I'm going now. Don't bother coming with me.'

She turned and hurried down the street, into the shadows, leaving me to think about the consequences of my decisions. I'd chosen what I thought was my patriotic duty over the girl I loved.

Chapter Nineteen

Britain declared war on Germany on August the fourth 1914 and all the chat about war as being a distant and unlikely possibility was instantly banished. Soon there was a call for all eligible men of Sheffield to enrol as a matter of urgency. I remember seeing the first recruitment poster on the second of September.

Two days later, having informed the management at Gibbs of our intention to volunteer, I was one of twenty-five young men who strolled down London Road, up The Moor, and into the Town Hall.

I wouldn't say that it was an anti-climax exactly, but I had imagined that there would have been more of a ceremony or at least a fanfare or two. Instead, we filled in a form and were told that we'd receive a postcard informing us of the date of our medical. The whole damn thing took a few minutes and then it was back to work, like nothing had happened.

'Is that it?' asked George Spears.

Only a few of the blokes I knew had a girlfriend, and I was the only one who was actively planning to get married. Our Joe had been courting a lass from somewhere up Crookes way, but she'd lost interest when he told her that he'd joined up. Joe said that she had told him that she'd never marry a soldier because she couldn't cope with the day-to-day stress of wondering if he was safe and the prospect of losing him. The door wasn't completely closed, because she'd asked him to call on her when it was all over and she might be "minded" to continue the relationship. I was worried that Annie might start to think the same way.

I need not have worried. Annie took a week off work and seemed to want to cling tighter to me that she'd ever done before. We'd go for longer and longer walks and many times we'd say nothing for an hour and, when we did speak, we would say the same thing together.

I remember the last Sunday before I left. After walking for hours, we ended up tired and thirsty, in the plague village of Eyam. I bought some bottles of beer and we sat for an hour in the village square, watching people going about their daily business. With it being a Sunday, people emerged from their stone built cottages and walked up the hill to the church, in much the same way that generations of villagers must have done for a thousand years. It seemed so serene and natural to see people, old and young, in their Sunday best, enjoying each other's company in the warmth of that early autumn morning. I don't imagine that many people we saw on that day could have imagined the horrors that were awaiting their young men.

Annie wanted to look around the churchyard at the graves of the villagers who had died when the plague hit the village. When it arrived, the plague had no respect for age or status and took the lives of anyone it could get, in much the same way as a bullet or a shell won't discriminate as to who they kill or whose heart is broken.

Annie stopped in front of one grave and said, 'Look read this… nine members of the same family died from the plague. Thomas 26th September 1665, Mary 30th September 1665, Elizabeth 1st October 1665, James 20th December 1665 and all the others too. When I come here again, I've got to bring them some flowers.'

After another drink, we walked down the hill into Grindleford and eventually caught a train back to Sheffield. On the way back we talked about where we'd get married and who we'd invite (as well as who we would not want to be there). Any wedding reception would have to be a modest affair due to the shortage of money. Annie's sister would be the single bridesmaid, and I'd ask Our Joe to be my best man. Annie's family had always attended St John's Church on Park Hill and she said that's where she'd like to get married, particularly as her father's funeral had been held in that church, and he would have approved.

As for when we'd marry, we both thought that we should wait until I'd left the army, which we hoped would be in less than six months, but if that was not possible we'd try to arrange the wedding for when I was on leave. While I was away Annie would save as much money as she could and make as many of the arrangements as possible. Before any of this we would have to prepare ourselves to be apart.

Chapter Twenty

Joe and I received identical postcards on September 9th. Both of us stood and read:

'You are requested to attend at the Corn Exchange on Thursday, the 10th inst. between the hours of 8a.m. and 1p.m. for Medical Inspection and Attestation.
By Order,
E.A MARPLES
Captn. and Acting Adjutant.'

'Are you going to tell mother, or shall I?' was my response, when he'd finished.

Mother came downstairs. She'd been listening and, typically of her, was trying to look busy and unconcerned, while barely managing to hold in her emotions,

'So that's it then. My two boys are leaving me, to fight against someone else's sons. It's the end of our family as we've known it.'

Our Joe tried to reason with her, but she wouldn't let him. 'Mother, we've been through this… '

'Be quiet Joe! You've no idea what this is doing to your dad and me. Do you know where Dad is? I'll tell you where he's gone, he's taken off by himself for a walk down the canal side to try and calm down, because he's terrified of losing you. Not just one of you, that'd be bad enough, but both of his sons. As for you Bill, you're not just leaving us, but you're abandoning Annie as well. How's she going to manage? That poor girl!'

I tried to find something to say, but all I could do was look at the floor and remind myself why I'd volunteered.

Mother went into the kitchen and slammed the door behind her.

***

Saying farewell to Annie proved to be as bad as anything that was to come. On the Sunday before I left I must have made a dozen efforts to walk down Loxley Hill, before stopping and going back to the farm gate, to kiss her and say goodbye one more time. Mr and Mrs Truswell had promised me that they'd take care of her and that the farm cottage would be ours, when we needed it. The Truswells had lost their only daughter, Ellen, to TB eleven years before and had grown to love Annie like she was their own. It was Mrs Truswell who eventually came to our rescue, by coming to the gate and gently guiding Annie back inside the house, so I could start the walk home and prepare for the morning.

The following morning, Our Joe and I took a tram into town and before walking through the door of the Corn Exchange he turned and shook my hand, 'Well, little brother, here we are at last. Ready to do our bit and to serve the nation. Let's promise to look after each other and to have some fun, when we can.'

Once inside, we had a medical examination (which revealed no physical impairments in either of the Farrells) before taking an oath of allegiance. I remember that the oaths were administered by some very serious looking officers, both with ruddy cheeks and a resplendent moustache. I then signed an acceptance document in which I swore to be faithful to King George the Fifth and his heirs and successors. After that, it was "as you were" and the Gibbs lads gathered outside.

'Well, that was easy enough!' someone said.

'I'm surprised they let a short-arse like you join up!' someone joked.

'Fancy a pint anyone?

Needless to say, quite a few pints were consumed during the rest of that afternoon at the Old Queen's Head, as we chatted excitedly about what was to come and what adventures awaited us. The only certainty was that we were required to turn up on Monday 14th September at Norfolk Barracks on Edmund Road, where, for us, the preparation for war would begin.

Chapter Twenty-One

Many years later, after Annie died, I found some of the letters we exchanged after I'd volunteered. It took me months to find the strength to read them (and when I did, it was always through tears). We had been told to avoid giving away any important information when writing home, so we had to be careful as to what went in our letters.

6ᵗʰ December 1914

Darling Annie,

How are you? I hope that you are well, my beautiful girl. I miss you so much that it hurts. I can't wait until we get our first leave and I can see you again and hold you tightly once more. Your face is the last thing I see when I close my eyes to go to sleep and it's the first thing I see when I wake up. I feel sorry for the other blokes, because they can't possibly have anyone as lovely as you. How are your mum and grandma? Well, I hope. Please give my regards to Mr and Mrs Truswell. Hope they're getting the cottage ready!

We've spent the last few weeks in the Norfolk Barracks, doing basic drilling and getting used to army life and yesterday was the BIG day, when we marched up to our new camp. It's in some woods above the city and I swear that on a clear day, I can see your house. It was absolutely FREEZING when we arrived; even some of the tougher blokes were struggling. It's quite nice up here; there are some big reservoirs and also lots of birds and wild animals. I would expect that some of the rabbits will find themselves on our plates before long!

The rumours are that we will soon start trench warfare training, out on the moors. Some of the blokes say that we'll also have to dig the trenches first, which seems a bit rough to me.

Anyway, I'm not good at writing letters so please forgive my poor spellings. I'll write again as soon as I can.

Your ever loving,

Bill.

PS George sends his love!

3rd April 1915

My Sweetheart,

Thank you for your letter, it always makes my day to hear from you. I'm sorry darling, but I have some bad news to share, and it is best if I tell you straight away. My Grandma passed away yesterday, in the Royal Infirmary. She went quietly in her sleep, and mum and I were with her at the end. The only consolation is that she is no longer suffering and that her pain has ended. Mum is upset, of course, but like me, she hated to see Grandma so poorly. Mum has decided to go and do some work in a factory, to help the war effort. She seems totally determined to do it!

Anyway, how are you? Hopefully, it should be getting a bit warmer up on the moors and I hope you are taking care of yourself. I'm glad that you have made so many friends and that you seem to want to protect each other. My only wish is that you could be here with me, rather than with them. All I can do is to try and keep busy, so that my mind isn't constantly worrying about you. Mrs Truswell sometimes has to tell me to stop working and take a rest, but every time that I do, all I can see is your smile. Please take care, my gorgeous Billy.

I often call in to see your parents. As usual, your mum puts on a brave face and tries not to show how worried she is. Just like me, she keeps busy and tries to take her mind off what's going on. She's looking forward to our wedding, as am I. Your dad is very quiet and sometimes it's hard to get him to say much at all.

I must end now, but never forget how much I love you. Promise me that you won't do anything silly with those guns. Say hello to Joe and give George a big kiss from me.

With all my love,

Annie.

19th December 1915

Beautiful Annie,

I hope that you are well, my angel. It was wonderful to see you last week and to spend precious time with you. When I said that you get more beautiful every time I see you, it's true. I was joking, when I said that I didn't like those new shoes. They are lovely and they suit you perfectly! I like what you've done to your hair as well. Speaking of hair, we have a bloke who cuts our hair and he must be a butcher by trade because there's hardly any left when he's done with us. I'm practically bald now!

Please don't worry, but this might be the last letter for a little while. We're now at Devonport and will be sailing somewhere tomorrow. I honestly don't know where we're going. The rumours are that our destination is Turkey or possibly the Far East. I wish they'd tell us, but obviously things like this are kept secret until the last minute. I expect we'll know soon enough.

The spirit among the blokes is always high and it's strange that while we come from so many different backgrounds, we all get on so well. We had a new bloke transferred into our section yesterday, who owns a bakery. All he wants to talk about is flour and yeast! He's already got the nickname 'Self Raising Stan'.

Most of us are just regular blokes, like me and Our Joe. We're ready to go and fight now and all the training has been done. I'll be careful though, so please don't worry my darling.

Goodbye for now and I'll write to you as soon as I can. I've just been told that we sail at four in the morning, so I'd better get my head down.

Love you always,

Bill.

Chapter Twenty-Two

Our first destination turned out to be Alexandria, in Egypt, and we had barely got ashore when we were told that we would soon be heading for Port Said, which was a thirteen hour train journey away. Some of the blokes were disappointed, because there seemed like no end of fun to be had in the back-streets of the port. There were the most exotic bars and girls that any of us had ever seen. Local men tried to lure us into dark backrooms, with the promise of 'endless pleasure.'

'You like our ladies English soldier? Come inside and try. Cheap drinks. Much relaxing.' seemed to be the standard welcome.

While we waited for our train to arrive, one or two of the blokes went inside these places and came out an hour later, looking pale and without any money left. I found somewhere quiet and wrote letters to Annie. I suppose that I sensed that this trip to Egypt was only delaying the inevitable and I wanted to let her know that I was safe. For now. We spent a couple of months by the Suez Canal, digging trenches and fortifications against a possible attack by the Turkish army, but by the end of February the decision had been taken to redeploy us to the battlefields of France.

It was only as the coast of Southern France emerged from the haze that I began to have the first twinges of trepidation that this would soon become serious and that I would soon see action. Our Joe stood next to me on the ship's rail as we edged into Marseille and we shared a few laughs about what we'd seen so far. It was clear that we were both trying to hide our fear as to what lay ahead, and after the jokes had blown away into the wind, Joe turned to me and said, 'Don't forget what I said to you, our kid, I'm always there for you.'

'Same here, Joe.'

We disembarked in Marseille and set off on a short march to the railway station, to begin our northerly journey through France, to a place from which many of us would never return home again. We were deposited in nothing less than goods wagons, with straw on the floor and without toilets or windows.

'Sit there you lot!' shouted an NCO, 'and if you're lucky, we'll stop for a pee in a few hours.'

'Is this it?' I asked.

'What do you want Farrell, bleedin' waitress service? This is war son. Get used to it. You'll be wishin' that you was back here before long, mark my words. Now get in and sit down!'

A range of farm animal noises came from up and down the train as we pulled out of Marseille and rolled across the fertile plains of Provence.

'Where we going?' asked Arthur Wortley, as he peered through a crack in the wooden carriage and out at the French countryside rushing past us.

'How do I know?' snapped Peter Long. 'Get back to kip!'

This kind of chat went on for much of the journey and ceased only when we fell asleep.

'Here Longy,' said Arthur, soon after waking up, 'what was it like in that bar in Egypt?'

'Wouldn't you like to know, my ginger-haired friend. Wouldn't you just like to know. Well I would describe it as... warm and welcoming.'

'Cor blimey!' said Arthur, going cross-eyed, with his tongue hanging out.

'Yes, indeed, Arthur my son. When this lot is over, I shall be returning to collect my receipt.'

Once or twice, we stopped at some small railway station in the middle of nowhere to use a toilet and to take a walk up the platform. On one occasion I was able to find Our Joe. He said that he was in a wagon with two older blokes, both of whom had seen action before, many years ago and, they'd heard rumours that we were definitely heading for the Somme. Either way, we were travelling north and we'd now left the warm south of France. Above us were leaden skies.

Sometime in the afternoon of March 18th, our train wheezed its way to a halt at a station in Pont Remy, after which we marched in stages towards the Somme. On arrival, one of the less pleasant NCOs, Sergeant Young, took pleasure in telling us, 'Tomorrow, you start repairin' and diggin' and I don't mean planting onions!'

Trench maintenance and "digging in" took several weeks and no one was spared the pain of moving mountains of mud. Because we were close to a river, with a high water table, the ground was particularly boggy, so, when it rained, the sides of the trenches would simply crumble. In order to support the sides of the trenches, we stacked up hundreds of sandbags against the inside of each trench and laid endless sheets of duckboard under foot (which eventually became flooded up to ankle height). The sides of the trenches were so high that the only way to see over the top was to use a periscope. I was never that keen to look out across No Man's Land because I didn't want to see an enemy soldier charging towards me.

Our trenches were laid out in a number of horizontal lines, with communication trenches running vertically from front to back. At the rear was the reserve line where we went to rest after a period on duty, and where any new blokes were briefed before being sent into the trench system. As you moved further forward, you would find yourself in the support trench, where there was often a telephone signaller and a couple of officers, tasked with overseeing the attacks and reporting back to headquarters. At the front and facing No Man's Land, was the main fire trench or front line as we called it. This trench was dug in sections (or bays), so that if a shell or mortar hit one part of it, then the others would be left undamaged. Each trench line had the protection of barbed wire running along its full length. The duty that we all feared, was to be ordered to man the forward listening post, which protruded out into No Man's Land and which would always be the first to be attacked, if the enemy launched an assault.

Our time on the moors above Sheffield had prepared us, to some extent, for life in the trenches, but, even so, it was as bad as anyone had imagined. For a start we were living on top of each other and very soon the trench began to fill with discarded food. Rats were our constant companions and, after not washing for weeks, we were not much cleaner than them. Someone told me that the really fat rats had probably gorged themselves on the flesh of dead soldiers. Many of us quickly became infested with body lice and most of us had fleas in our hair. Flies buzzed around the human waste overflowing from the toilets. When I say "toilets" I actually mean a hole dug in the ground, with a plank of wood so sit on. The smell was… well perhaps that is best left to the imagination.

The routine that we were given consisted of four days on the front line, followed by four days in reserve and then four days resting. That was at least the idea, although it never really worked like that. There was never any actual time to relax, because we were always on alert for enemy attacks or having to dodge the shells that were randomly lobbed at us. Men were always required to go up front to repair barbed wire fences damaged by shells or to listen for noises in the night, which might indicate an attack across No Man's Land. There was always the danger of being shot by a sniper and we had been warned of the use of gas. Our particular system of warning for a gas attack was not complicated: it was simply someone banging on an empty shell case shouting "Gas! Gas!" It goes without saying that "keep yer bloody 'ead down" became like a religious mantra, along with "don't go for a shit with too many other blokes or some German will drop a grenade on yer noggins and we don't want you to die with yer pants down!"

A normal day started at five in the morning, with the order "Stand-to," meaning wake up and prepare for an attack by the enemy. If nothing happened, after half an hour, we would get a rum ration, before standing down at six a.m. Breakfast, usually of tea and a rasher of bacon, would arrive at seven, after which we would be assigned various duties, such as maintaining weapons or removing rubbish from the trench. Those soldiers with specialist training would go about their duties. Dinner was served around noon, after which we might occasionally be allowed to relax for a few hours. Tea was at five thirty, followed by another "Stand-to" and further duties for the rest of the night. Some of the blokes had night duties such as getting stores or general maintenance of the trenches. I remember using what spare time I had writing to Annie and to my parents.

Our regiment had a command post on an elevated point in the landscape called "Fond de la voie de Epine," which I think means something like "high point from where you can see the mountains." George Spears and I were once ordered up there to help some lads finish the construction of the observation building, from where the commanders could see what was happening.

As we were having a tea break, George said, 'That's the River Somme over there, but I can't see any mountains.'

'I don't speak French, but that's just what I thought it meant. For all I know, it might mean something completely different. Anyway, let's enjoy being out of the trenches for a while. What's that over there?'

George and I could see a few houses and a church, about half a mile away across No Man's Land, and it was clear that something was going on over there. Fleets of trucks were moving in and out and there was far more activity than you'd expect in a small French village. I thought I'd ask Sergeant Fairburn who had been put in charge of us for the day,

'Sarge! What's going on in that village?'

'Them's the Germans,' laughed Fairburn. 'They're digging in and preparing to fight, the same as us, you daft sod! They've got that village and our top brass need to control this area, so sooner or later it'll all kick off and we get stuck into 'em. That's what we're here for, isn't it? It's not a ruddy holiday. Now if you two don't mind, I'd like you to stop day dreaming and get on with some bloody work!'

Other than the occasional shell whizzing over us, things were quiet until the morning of Sunday April 4th. That was when the Germans really opened upon us for the first time. Our Joe and myself were sorting out a delivery of food supplies that had arrived overnight when all hell broke loose. Without warning, huge explosions rocked the trench, blowing us all off our feet. Mud and rocks rained down as we scrambled to cover our heads. I found myself under a pile of earth, struggling to breathe as my nose and mouth were full of mud.

Around me, as I scrambled to escape from the darkness, I could hear a voice shouting, 'Down boys, down!' as more grenades thundered into the ground around us, each arrival preceded by its own deathly soprano note of bloody intent.

The entire attack must have lasted no more than a minute or two, and, when it was over, as we each staggered to our feet, the sight that met us was one of horror. Men lay around us, many bleeding from wounds to their legs and heads and I could hear cries for help coming from beneath mounds of soil and mud. Someone called for shovels to be brought, so that we could start digging them out, but by the time the shovels arrived, we'd already dug most of them out by hand.

I don't know how many men were injured in that attack; only that one of my mates, Alex McKenzie was killed. He was officially the first of us to die as a result of enemy action. Only a bloody stain in the mud marked the spot where a few minutes earlier he'd been standing next to me, telling jokes. I wish that had been the only time that any of us were to see someone's guts spilling into the open air. It was hours before anyone spoke again.

I'm going to stop and let you think about where you want to go from here. You have two choices. You can either forget about all of this, and go back to your own life, or, if it's what you really want, you can be one of us and see what was to follow. Just remember that if you decide to come with us, it'll be unpleasant. I'll know what you want to do.

Chapter Twenty-Three

As Bill's voice faded away, I found myself standing at Joe's grave. The only movement around me was when an indolent breeze disturbed the tops of the trees, before disappearing across the featureless farmland.

For a moment or two I seemed to be neither in 1916 or 1972, but rather somewhere in between. Everyone I'd met from the past had seemed so real to me that I felt as if they'd been part of my everyday life. I'd been with Annie as we ambled through High Hazels Park and I'd walked to Loxley to see her.

'Matty… Thank God you're here. Where the hell have you been? I've been running about everywhere looking for you. I'm responsible for you.'

Andrew was striding through the archway, looking relieved to see me.

'I've been standing here,' I replied.

'Come on, be honest. I've been in here once already and you were definitely not there. That shell case that you're holding was lying on the grass, but there was no sign of you.'

I tried to change the subject, after all, how could I explain where I'd been?

'Have you seen Great Uncle Joe's grave?'

'I noticed it, but I was so concerned about you that I didn't stop to look for long.'

'Well, here it is Andrew and, look: there's Peter Long and Arthur Wortley.'

'How do you know their names? They only have initials on the grave.'

I wanted to tell him that I knew that Longy had been to a seedy club in Alexandria and that Arthur had ginger hair and could go cross-eyed, but Andrew would have thought that I was mad.

'Just a guess,' I said.

We paused at the grave of Alex McKenzie, 'Poor bloke, similar age to me.' Andrew sighed.

'I know. Bill was standing next to him when he was hit by a rifle grenade.'

'Oh really? Come on let's go and have something to eat. We've only got one more day before we have to head home. I thought we'd walk up to Luke Copse cemetery and then have a quick look in Queen's and Serre Road on the way back. I've sort of had enough of looking at these places now.'

'These other cemeteries are where you'll find the Accrington Pals. They were in the centre and to the right of the line, whereas Bill and the Sheffield lads were on the left flank.'

'There you go again. Anyone would have thought that you were there. You've done your homework that's for sure.'

We did what we said we'd do and paused for a while, in each of the tiny cemeteries, before going back to the campsite, to prepare our last evening meal prior to setting off home in the morning.

Later that evening, as we sat around the campfire, Andrew asked me what had been my favourite part of the trip. I said that I had loved walking around Ypres and especially looking at the museum, but that those few moments as the bugler played the Last Post at the Menin Arch were the best. It had been a good few days, but I'd soon go back to the reality of hoping that Amanda would get better and that we could be a complete family again. Andrew was of course oblivious of the fact that I'd met Bill and Annie and that I had the chance of one last opportunity to learn how Bill earned the medal. I'd decided that I would ask Bill to show me what happened next and I trusted that he'd look after me.

'Before we set off, I'd like to have one last visit to see Our Joe.'

'That's fine; just don't go wandering off again that's all. The ferry doesn't leave until three-thirty and so we've got loads of time to pack everything up and have a last look around, before we set off to Calais.

'Thanks, Andrew. I'm off to bed now.'

'I'll be there myself in a few minutes, once I've finished this drink.'

I snuggled into my sleeping bag for the last time, secure in the knowledge that my next sleep, would be back in my own bed. Andrew crawled into the tent and was soon snoring next to me. As I closed my eyes, I told Bill that I was ready to face the past and see for myself what had taken place, just a few yards from where I was. From far away, the cacophony of voices returned and, once again, I stepped into Bill's boots.

Chapter Twenty-Four

In a trench, nothing was ever private. On one occasion, I was attempting to shave, using a cracked mirror, balanced awkwardly on my knee. I'd nicked my chin with the blunt razor blade and was trying to stem the trickle of blood, with a dirty rag, 'Bloody hell George, how is a handsome bloke like me, meant to preserve his good looks under these conditions?'

'I wouldn't bother if I was you,' he said. 'Annie won't mind the odd scratch.'

As I shaved, George looked at me through the mirror. 'I want to ask you something,' I said,

'Ask away, Private Farrell.'

'If… you know… the worst happened to me, will you go and visit Annie and try to take care of her.'

George could tell that I was serious.

'Yes, of course. She's special, not that you don't already know it, but it's true. As we're being honest with each other, do you know that I once asked her out?'

'She told me.'

'I did, but I never stood a chance with you around. I overheard Joe, talking to some of the lads at work about you fancying her and that was it. Speaking of Joe, where is he?'

'Running an errand for Fairburn, I think he's trying to get into his good books. God knows why. He'll be back soon.'

'Anyway, in answer to your question: yes, I'll make sure that she's looked after, but let's not think about it, eh? I still think the Germans will chicken out and that we'll be home soon and you two can get married.'

I was unconvinced by his optimism and was now sticking a piece of newspaper onto my chin to stem the blood.

'I hope you're right Spearsie, boy. I hope you're right. I'll write to her later… what's that you're reading?'

George was holding a magazine that someone had brought into the trench and then discarded.

'It's this new magazine for the lads in the trenches. It's called the Wipers Times.'

'Wipers? What's that mean?'

George said that "Wipers" was a deliberate misspelling of "Ypres" and that the magazine was intended to cheer us all up, with a blend of poems, gallows humour and mock adverts. It had its own vocabulary, which only British soldiers understood, for example, if an article referred to a "Flying Pig" then it meant a British mortar grenade or if an "FM" said anything, then that referred to a Field Marshall.

'Let me finish it and I'll let you have it. It's got poetry in it,' said George.

The idea of reading poetry filled me with disgust and I made it clear that I had no intention of ever reading poetry again.

'Poetry? I hate that stuff. I was never any good at it… Shakespeare and all that. Why don't they write it in proper English? I wandered lonely as… can't remember the rest.'

George took the opportunity to annoy me by reading the poem of the week,

'So what do you think of this? It's been sent in by Corporal K Ringrose of the Accrington Pals, and is entitled "The Field." He cleared his throat, took on a dramatic pose, straightened his helmet and began:

The child who daydreams in the fields of his imagination
Should only dream of pretend battles, fought in the gentle meadows of home.
The touch of a friend should only be a hearty "well done!"
rather than the tearing open of the battle dress
to stem the flow of blood from his wounds,
with cries of agony as his heart surrenders to the darkness ahead.

What hope has he, if one day, he must exchange the country lanes of childhood,
for the battle-stained purgatory of a muddy grave?
To lay forever beneath the alien soil of an unfamiliar field?
The only consolation, is that those left behind will know,
that his soul is now free to ride the breezes and accompany the swallows to new fields,
On their journey into the sun.'

There was silence, as everyone around us seemed to be thinking about how to respond to the poem. After several seconds, I said, 'Nope! Still hate poetry. I didn't understand a bloody word of it. In fact, I can honestly say that I hate reading. I can read of course, but to me, it's just dead time and I could be doing something else. Like playing sport, for example.'

'What I don't get,' said Joe, who by now was sitting between Peter and George, 'is why people actually feel the need to write poetry at all. Why don't they just use normal words, like everyone else does? Poetry is just showing off.'

There was a murmur of agreement from all around.

'I disagree completely!'

We all turned in astonishment to look at Private Boulby, who had been listening quietly, from where he'd been sitting on a muddy step.

'What did you say Boulby?' I asked.

'Well, I see it like this,' Boulby continued, with a faraway look on his face, 'nothing else allows a person to express emotions, more beautifully than through poetry and literature. Think about rhyme and rhythm and how the great poets like Shelley and John Donne weave their imagery for effect, or how a great writer of fiction can paint a picture using language to stir the emotions, with a single sentence. Where would we be without poetry and fiction? It's like making music with words rather than notes. Literature is what separates us from the heathens.'

No one could quite take in what they'd just heard. Boulby was forty-three, and old enough to be our father. He was about as quiet a bloke as you could ever meet and on occasions you would notice him lingering shyly in the background, listening in to the conversations. It's not that he was unpleasant in any way at all, in fact, when he did say anything it was often funny and he could reduce us all to tears of laughter with a sarcastic comment. One or two of the NCOs had tried to bully him because he was obviously better educated than them, but Boulby just ignored them and did his job.

'Remind us what do you do in civvy life, Boulby?' Joe asked.

'I'm a master at a preparatory school ... I also write poetry.'

Chapter Twenty-Five

May arrived and the weather dried up a little, although a late frost on one night had some of the sentries hopping about trying to keep warm. Our unit, which included George, Joe, Boulby and I, were due to go on reserve in a week or so, and were counting down the days. There had been sporadic shelling from the German lines and the odd sniper had caused some alarm, but generally speaking things were quiet.

Something in what Boulby had said about poetry had made me think about life and the definition of love. I tried to work out exactly what it was, but the best that I could come up with was that I loved Annie so much that my letters in themselves did not seem adequate enough to express how I felt about her. I began to think that I should try to say how I felt in a different way and perhaps poetry might help me to express my thoughts on a higher level. When I was sure that no one else was around I started to try and write some (simple) poetry using rhyme and attempting to compare her eyes to this and her lips to this or that. I'd usually laugh at my own rather pathetic effort and throw it away.

Boulby asked me one evening what it is that I had been trying to write and why I kept screwing it up and throwing it away. Looking around to ensure that we were alone, I asked, 'Boulby. I want to try and write some poetry to Annie. When I've written some, would you mind having a look at it for me?'

'Of course. Before you do, can I tell you what I try to teach my boys?'

'Yes, please.'

'The more that you read and absorb poetry, the better you become at writing it. Don't try to be Tennyson straight away, but think about developing your own style and way of expressing your feelings. Do you know the most important thing about writing poetry?'

'What is it?'

'Be honest with yourself. It doesn't matter what anyone thinks, just say what's in your heart and that's all that matters. Read this.'

He passed a slim, hardback book over to me, taking care to ensure that no one could see the transfer take place.

'What is it?'

'It's a collection of Shakespeare's sonnets. Take it away and read a few. Look especially at Sonnet twenty-nine: that's my favourite.'

'What am I looking for? And what's a sonnet?'

'A sonnet is a particular type of poem that was popular in Shakespeare's time. The beauty of sonnets is that a skilled poet can really say a lot in a short space of time, just fourteen lines to be exact. Just read it and you'll see that Shakespeare thinks about many of the sad things that he has experienced, like having few friends or no money, and then he remembers his lover and he realises that nothing else matters except her, so the rest can go to hell. He doesn't care about anyone but her. Isn't that how you feel about Annie?'

'Yes, I suppose it is.'

We could see Our Joe approaching and so I slipped Boulby's book under my coat and Boulby got up and left as if nothing of any importance had been spoken between us.

I took Boulby at his word and, over the next few days and weeks, when the coast was clear, I read as many of the sonnets as I could and number twenty-nine in particular. I'm not saying that I understood every word of every sonnet, but Shakespeare inspired me into having a go and writing some poetry to Annie and by doing so I hoped that I had taken my expressions of love to a higher level.

One evening, after tea, George sidled up to me and asked me what Boulby and I had been talking about.

'Now then Farrell, some of the lads have noticed that you and Boulby have been having little chats. What's going on?'

'Boulby's fine once you get to know him,' I said. 'He's bloody clever and knows a lot about stuff. If you want to know, I want to impress Annie by writing her a poem and I thought I'd show it to him first.'

'You? Writing poetry? After all you said about hating it? Poetry!'

'Shut up! I don't want them all knowing. It's just that when Boulby said all that about how poetry can help with expressing emotions, it got me thinking about life and what happens after.'

'My God! I don't believe it!'

'What don't you believe?'

'You! Being interested in writing and all that.'

'Well, I am now. Do you want a look at what I've written? I'm going to post it to Annie tomorrow and if the worst happens to me, she'll know that I wasn't a total idiot.'

George thought about it for a moment, but decided that it really should remain private between us, 'No thanks mate. Let her be the first to read it. Anyway, here comes Joe, so let's change the subject; he'll die laughing if he finds out.'

Chapter Twenty-Six

When you've lived in a sludge-filled slit in the ground for months, combing nits out of your hair and peeling lice from your skin, you can sometimes lose track of days and dates, so I'm unsure as to whether this was May 15th or 16th. Our unit had been in reserve at the rear of the trench lines for a few days and we had been simply enjoying having some space to move around, before having to go back to becoming rats in a sewer. That isn't to say that rest periods were simply rest and nothing else, that isn't true. We were sent out on route marches and were drilled in individual skills, such as advancing under fire and in the use of Lewis guns. We rehearsed attacks on enemy lines and various specialists were drilled in wire cutting and communications.

Nobody expects the enemy to send a telegram warning of an attack, but, when it came, the accuracy and deadliness of their artillery must have caught even the most alert of us by surprise. It arrived with the ferocity that up to now had been missing. Starting at two in the morning, wave after wave of Howitzers opened up and their accuracy was lethal. When the earth around you is erupting from the pounding of heavy armaments, there's little you can do, other than to lay flat and hope that you're not right underneath one. During one brief pause in the attack, I raised my head over the top of the trench for a few seconds and, I saw what I've always imagined hell to look like. Huge craters, some five yards wide and almost as deep, had been carved out of the earth around us. Acrid smoke was now drifting across us and, worst of all, I could see lifeless figures lying scattered like discarded toys across a child's bedroom. I tried to count them, but it was clear that some blokes were in several pieces.

This curtain remained only open for a few seconds, before the barrage started again. Every screaming shell was echoed by the screams of terror around me. I could hear what sounded like blokes calling for their mothers through blood filled mouths. Some voices were calling out to God or Jesus for help, but they were deaf to any cries for mercy. On and on it went and the shells continued to pound us.

Eventually, the shelling stopped, leaving a wasteland of broken bodies and trenches. A period of silence followed, before voices started to bark out orders:

'Get up here with stretchers!' or 'Where are the bloody medics?'

The first face I saw was George.

'Have you seen Joe?' I asked.

'No. He was near me when it started, but I don't know where he is now.'

'Help me find him!'

No sooner had we turned to face where we thought he'd been than we saw him helping to carry a stretcher from up front. When he saw us we could see that this was no time for any smiles of recognition. Joe turned to us, his eyes wide with shock and his uniform drenched in fresh blood, 'You two get up there; there's loads of injured lads. I'll see you later.'

George and I clambered over the rubble of what had been the support trench and found that there was virtually nothing left up front. The trench itself was unrecognisable and all that was left of it was a series of pits carved out by shellfire. Each hole contained dead and injured men and I knew every one of them. We lowered ourselves down into each shell hole and disentangled the living from the dead. One by one, we carefully helped the walking wounded to a medic or got the most badly injured onto a stretcher and carried him to the hospital tent. This took an hour before our attention turned to removing the dead. I threw up when I lifted the first one on to a stretcher, but after that we learned to detach ourselves from the sight of human remains. As we carried each one away I thought about how I knew him and how we'd met. Some were classmates at school, others were lads I'd played football with or against. In the end we learned to simply not look down at each load that we carried and to concentrate only on making sure that we gave him as much dignity as possible. That was spoiled by the sight of the dead being loaded onto a cart and driven away, like sacks of rubbish being taken to the dump.

After the last of the dead and injured had been taken away, George looked at me wearily and said, 'I need something strong to drink. I've got some rum hidden away, so let's get away from this madness for a while.'

And so we sat outside our tent and rested for a few minutes as the sun rose, trying to take in what we'd been through. Around us the task of rebuilding our smashed trenches had already started and we knew that before long someone would order us to get up, grab a spade and start shifting dirt once more.

Sergeant Dorrell, who on most occasions we hated as a bullying little toad, limped past us, bleeding from a wound on his thigh, and I felt compelled to ask him if he was OK, 'You hurt Sarge?'

On most occasions, any attempt to engage with Dorrell on a personal level would be met with some kind of sarcasm and personal abuse, but on that morning he looked like a broken man, 'Spears? Farrell? You two all right?'

'Yes, Sarge,' I replied. 'We were in reserve when it started and we've been manning the stretchers ever since. What happened?'

'They raided the front line trenches, under cover of the shellfire. Most of the lads up front were on their own, and the raiding party were in our trenches before they knew it and all they could do was fight hand to hand. They did their best until support arrived, but by then it was too late for a few.'

'Christ almighty!'

'I'd say at a guess we've got a dozen dead and perhaps fifty wounded. Anyway, I'm going to get this leg looked at. By the time I get back, I want you two back at work. Get it?'

'Yes, Sarge. We're going back now.'

Once Dorrell had gone we got back to work, shifting mud and replacing the stinking trenches with some more filthy rat-runs for us to live in. That is until the next action, which for many of us would be the last.

Chapter Twenty-Seven

I have always supposed that the generals, up there in their command post, would have been given details of how many men were killed or injured, although we, the living, were just expected to pick ourselves up and get on with it. The list of missing faces told its own story and there were quite a few lads who we never saw again. Among them were a couple of my cricket team-mates, Jack Firth and Horace Renshaw, two of the nicest blokes you could ever know. Jack was more than just an acquaintance: he was my second cousin. We'd met at many family occasions and had always got on well. I was the person who had first told him about the army recruitment drive and had suggested that he should join up with the rest of us.

The whispers up and down the trenches were that the Accrington Pals had borne the brunt of the casualties and in the end that turned out to be true, although no one was free from the pain and shock of losing friends. But, as is often the case after a traumatic experience, we concentrated on work as a way of hiding from grief and anxiety. Our lines urgently needed rebuilding and that kept us busy for a few weeks, with little time for rest and recreation.

Once the repairs were completed, we began to practise for the forthcoming assault on Serre, and all those frozen days up on the moors, clambering out of practice trenches, began to make sense. There were more route marches and more simulated attacks on enemy lines, involving the cutting of the wire and taking out their forward listening points. By mid-June, we were impatient to get it over and starting to become restless.

On Saturday 24th June, our heavy artillery started to pound the German lines and it was obvious that we'd soon be on our way. The bombardment lasted four days and its aim must have been to destroy their defences, in the same way as ours had been flattened.

Then the rain came and all we could do was to sit and wait, as the mud in our trench became stickier and water ran down our faces.

'Right lads,' said Dorrell, 'go and get some kip. We'll be needed on standby at 03:45 tomorrow morning. You all know what to do by now.'

'So it's to be on the first of July 1916,' someone said.

'It's as good a day to die as any other!'

Chapter Twenty-Eight

People have asked me, what it was like to be about to climb out of a trench and face the possibility of imminent death. My reply has always been to say that the answer is to be found in the faces of the lads as we lined up and prepared to move forward and up the steps into No Man's Land. My mates and I were due over the top in the in the first wave and I remember, some were ashen faced with fear, while others attempted to present an air of optimism and even enthusiasm for what was to come. Some faces gave nothing away about how they were feeling. Next to me, I saw someone slip a letter into his tunic pocket and pat it down as if it might try to escape. I recall wondering how my family and friends might remember me and what they'd say about me if I was killed. I think I'd been in a church twice in my life, but I found myself promising God that if he spared me, then I'd try and do something positive with my life. Needless to say, he's still waiting. From behind, Joe patted me on the shoulder and said, 'You'll be all right little brother. I'll keep an eye on you!'

Those few minutes, as I we lay waiting for the signal to get up and move forwards, were without doubt, the longest of my life, before at seven-thirty the bombardment halted and a whistle sounded, signalling the start of our advance. An eerie early morning mist shrouded No Man's Land and I remember how the thick mud began to stick to my boots as I lurched forward, rifle in hand. Then the German machine gunners started doing their deadly work. The bloke next to me fell to the ground, instantly dead, his head having taken a direct hit. I looked along the line and lads were seemingly being hit from the side as well as from directly ahead. I thought I'd be hardened to the sound of agony and mutilation, but I was not ready to hear familiar voices screaming in terror as their lives ebbed away. The worst thing was being unable to help them as self-preservation became the over-riding desire, and if I could see those blokes again I'd never stop apologising to them.

As if the number of casualties had jolted him into action, an officer bellowed an order for us to get down to the floor, leaving me able only to see the soles of some bloke's boots as he lay in front of me.

The order to "stay down" was repeated as other waves of men emerged from our trenches and hurried to join us, but still the enemy machine guns mowed them down in their dozens and by the time they'd reached us their numbers must have been cut by half.

'Up and forward!' the voice called above the hammering of the guns and so I pulled myself up and continued towards the German barbed wire lines in the distance. Our objective was shrouded by smoke, and in the noise and heat seemed to be receding rather than coming closer.

Men around me continued to fall and, more than once, I stumbled over a dead or wounded soldier and had to drag myself back to my feet, my lungs ablaze and my vision blurred by perspiration and dirt. I was one of the first to reach the German wire fencing, and much to my horror it was largely undamaged and looked like it hadn't been cut. I reached for my wire cutters but all I could see were exhausted men arriving through the haze and in no condition to go much further.

'Let's get back, we're going nowhere today!' yelled the newly arrived Fairburn and so we began the hurried retreat back to our trenches. This time however, we were now under fire from behind and once again I could hear the sickening thud of bullets hitting blokes and the cries of agony coming from everywhere around me. To my right, Fairburn took one in the guts and was dead before I had the chance to get to him.

I was within reach of our trench, when I heard a voice from somewhere in the swirling smoke, 'Over here someone. Help me get this bloke back.'

After squirming, worm-like, through puddles of mud and blood, I crawled into a shell-hole within which George was kneeling beside a dead soldier.

'He's dead,' I screamed over the rattling of machine guns. 'Leave him.'

'No, he isn't Bill. Look at him.'

When we rolled him over, we saw the face of a boy. It's difficult to come to any accurate guess as to his age, but to us he looked like he was no more than sixteen. Through the mud, his face could have easily been mistaken for that of a teenage girl, such was its freshness and innocence. He'd taken one in the neck. I took off my tunic and pressed it into the wound in an effort to stem the blood flow.

I wiped some mud from the boy's face and gripped his hand.

'What's your name, mate?'

'From somewhere, he found the strength to say, 'Ernest. Thanks for helping me, Bill.'

'Don't be daft,' I said, looking over at George. 'We'll sort you out, pal.'

The boy looked up, but was now unable to speak, and, during a lull in the gunfire, we managed somehow to carefully lift him and get him back into the trench. I can still remember his features twisted in pain and how his eyes rolled around as his lips moved noiselessly.

'Hey! We need a medic over here,' I called though among the chaos. No one answered, so I tried again. 'Please, somebody help this boy… please!'

A grim-faced doctor arrived, and a short time later the boy was taken away.

After the stretcher bearing Ernest had gone, I asked George if he'd seen him before.

'Never seen him in my life. The funny thing is… after we got the order to get back here, I ended up to my ankles in mud and my boot came off. Like an idiot, I stopped to try and get it back on and from nowhere, he came up behind me and asked me if I'd been hit. When I say he was behind me, that's exactly what I mean, he was between me and the German lines. I'd no sooner told him to get down, when he was hit. If he hadn't been there, I reckon I'd have taken it. I swear to God, that he smiled at me as he fell.'

I gathered myself again, before remembering what had been at the forefront of my mind, 'Have you seen Our Joe?'

'No. Not since we went over,' George answered.

'Help me find him!'

I suggested that George should search amongst the lads who were just getting back while I went and looked for Joe in the support trenches, in case he'd made it back and was resting. Such was the chaos around us, that Joe could have been anywhere.

The first face I recognised was Boulby. He was sitting, head bowed and shaking with exhaustion.

'Boulby mate! Are you hurt? Can I get you a drink?'

'No. Leave me alone please!'

'That's fine, I will. Just one thing, have you seen Joe Farrell?'

With what seemed like the remainder of his energy, Boulby lifted his head and looked up at me, his eyes reddened with sadness and fatigue, 'I'm pretty sure he was hit as we were trying to get back and I couldn't stop to help. Please tell him that I'm sorry.'

'Don't worry, I'll tell him when I see him.'

Boulby's head bowed again and he closed his eyes.

Having been told that Joe had been hurt, George and I spent the next however long frantically looking on stretchers, as men were carried away, but Joe was not among them. I then decided then that I should look for him among the dead and so I began to lift the blankets from the faces of the corpses in order to see if he was one of them. Some blokes had no face left, while the faces of others seemed to have an almost puzzled expression, but still no Joe. George came and tugged at my sleeve, 'Look, Bill. If Joe is injured then he might still be somewhere out there.'

'You're right, so I'm going back out there, Spearsie!'

'Don't be stupid. You'll get yourself killed as well… Can't you hear that they're still picking us off?'

Nothing anyone said after that made any difference. Blokes were still arriving back in the trenches and I remember asking a few if they'd seen Our Joe, but most were unable to speak, let alone give me a sensible answer. I picked up one of the many rifles that littered the trench floor and stepped back on the ladder and over the top.

I'd say that it was close to one in the afternoon and by then the enemy fire was no more than the occasional rap of a German sniper's rifle as he took aim at anyone still able to crawl back home. Head down, I bolted through lingering smoke to the nearest shell-hole, weaving between corpses, many partially buried in mud. Inside, I found nothing but a few bits of blood-soaked kit and a discarded helmet.

Had an enemy sniper seen me, then I knew that he'd be watching for me to emerge from the shell-crater, but such was the desire to find my brother that I no longer cared. It had to be worth the risk and so, with a silent prayer to a god in whom I had never truly believed, I crawled out and back into the wasteland.

I remember pushing past some more twisted remains, some barely recognisable as human, and forcing myself to push forward through puddles of still warm blood. In the lingering smoke, I had no bearings and around me hung the stench of decay, but I pushed on, calling Joe's name, without reply.

I'm told that at one o'clock, a truce had been agreed, between both sides, allowing for the rescue and retrieval of dead and injured, but I was unaware of this and continued to feel my way across the battlefield. All I recall seeing was what was left of the regiment, lying face down in defeat, when from close to me in the mist, I heard a voice, 'Bill is that you?'

'Who's there?' I called.

'It's me George. Have you found him?'

'No, I bloody haven't and I'm not giving in until I do.'

'Listen, we've only got half an hour out here, and we have to get some of these blokes back. I'm sorry but you've got to stop wasting time and think about these other lads. They've got families too. Come on Bill, he might be anywhere and he's probably looking for you, so let's get on with it!'

I couldn't really argue with him and, despite being desperate to continue, I saw the logic of what he was saying, so we spent as long as we could recovering what remained of the boys. I picked up anything that could be used to identify each body and that included watches, letters and rings. A few other blokes, carrying stretchers had joined us and we threw what body parts we could find onto the stretcher and got it back to our lines. It was only when I was handing over what I'd picked up, that I recognised Joe's wrist-watch among it all. The glass and watch face were smashed, but I'd seen it so often that I didn't have to think twice. I turned it over and Our Joe's initials were engraved on the back.

'Anyone know where this came from?' I asked somewhat feebly, but no one did and, besides which, who really cared?

As a footnote to that day, I remember that eventually I found Joe, or what remained of him. He was among the ranks of those taken away for burial in a small makeshift cemetery down the road. I don't know if Ernest survived or not. I asked around, but no one had any recollection of ever seeing a lad matching his description.

A few months later, I was awarded the Military Medal and my name was recorded in the London Gazette, which I think my dad cut out and pasted into a scrapbook. I've always had mixed feelings about the medal. Of course, it's nice to receive such an honour, but I'd swap it for my brother's life in a heartbeat.

Chapter Twenty-Nine

Following the disaster of July the first 1916, many of us who survived the attack were sent home on extended leave. George came to our house in order to pay his respects. The house itself was silent and full of fresh flowers that dad had grown on his allotment. A photograph of Joe, in his uniform, stood proudly on the mantelpiece. My father became a distant figure, preferring his own company. Mother became involved in the local church and became active in helping out with the care of disabled soldiers. Annie and I were married in October 1916, with George as the best man; although we all knew that Joe would have had the job in other circumstances. We had just about enough time to settle into our little cottage on Truswell's farm and start to build our lives together, before I went back and re-joined my regiment.

Our regimental history records show that after July the first 1916 "around 460 men and 15 officers were missing, wounded or killed," but the truth is that no one really knows for sure. Very few of us made it to the German front line trench, and when we did there was only death waiting to welcome us. The names of those who we never found were later carved on memorial stones and I took some comfort in the fact the Our Joe was given a gravestone of his own.

Following a new recruitment drive, our regiment was "re-stocked" and us "old blokes" found ourselves serving alongside a new batch of often young and enthusiastic recruits. The winter of 1916 and 1917 came close to breaking our spirit. It was well below freezing for months and the trenches were unbearable in those conditions. Hundreds of us were hospitalised with frostbite and the effects of extreme cold, in fact that's how George lost the tips of his fingers and was eventually discharged on medical grounds.

I stayed on and I'm proud to say that the lads never allowed their spirits to fall entirely, and by May 1917 we'd seen action on Windmill Spur, when we successfully fought off a German attack, and, despite heavy losses, we were also part of the successful attack at Oppy-Gavrelle. But as the war dragged on it began to take its toll on everyone and when we were gassed at the battle of Vimy Ridge in September 1917 it was said to have been the end of the Sheffield Battalion. Even today, the bones of our comrades are dragged up to the surface by tractors as farmers work the same land we occupied. Our mates are always re-buried with full military honours and, of course, we never forget them.

You must return to where you belong. I'd ask only that you remember what you've seen and experienced and use it positively. I knew that our paths were destined to cross again and that you deserved to see what happened. You may be surprised to know how all of this was possible, but we'll leave that for now.

Chapter Thirty

'Come on! Wake up sleepy head, we've got to pack up now and set off home.'

Andrew was gently shaking my sleeping bag as I opened my eyes, 'What year is it?' I mumbled.

Andrew began to laugh, 'It was 1972, when we went to sleep, so I'm sure that it's still 1972 now. That must have been quite a dream that you've been having. Come on, jump up. I've made us some breakfast. If you hurry up, you'll just have enough time to run up to the cemetery again.'

'No, I don't think I will.'

Andrew seemed puzzled, 'Are you sure? I thought you wanted to go one last time.'

'No, it's OK. I'll come back again one day.'

I'd learned everything that I wanted to know and the experience of being with Bill and the others, and above all I wanted to go home.

The journey home was uneventful enough, but, however much I tried, I could not push away the memories of what my senses had experienced during those weeks in 1916. In addition to seeing Amanda again, I wanted to see George, and find out what had done since the war, and if he could tell me anything about how Bill had adjusted to life after the war.

Andrew had called my parents from a telephone box near Derby in order to tell them that we'd be home in an hour, and as we pulled up at the bottom of our drive they came out of the house to meet us. Mum asked Andrew if he wanted to come inside for a cup of tea, but he said that he needed to get home in order to prepare to rejoin his regiment at the weekend.

'Well, Matty,' asked Dad as we went inside. 'What was it like?'

I told him where we'd been and that I'd found the Sheffield Memorial. Dad seemed interested, particularly when I told him that I'd found the grave of his great Uncle Joe.

'How sad… and all so young,' he said. 'I sometimes wonder how he died, and whether my Granddad was there. Anyway, Matty, go and get a bath and have a good night's sleep in your own bed. I expect you'll have missed it.'

'Yes, Dad. Oh, one thing.'

'Mmm?'

'Can I look at some of those letters that you found in the attic?'

'What, now?'

'Only for ten minutes Dad. There's something I wanted to find out. Please?'

Dad said that he'd bring them up to my room. Apparently he'd been meaning to read them, but, what with Amanda being in hospital, he hadn't got around to it.

I'd just climbed into bed, when Dad came in with the box of Bill's letters.

'Just a few minutes. Promise?'

'Yes, Dad. Promise. Are we going to see Amanda tomorrow?' I asked.

'Of course! Goodnight.'

I lifted the box onto the bed and took out the first of the letters.

June 20th 1916

Dearest darling, I hope that you are well,

I wanted to write to you again, because I think that we'll soon be ready for the off and you never know how things might turn out. I know I've often told you how much I love you, but this time, I want you to know more than ever. I'll come home, just as soon as I can and once I get there, I promise that I'll never leave you.

Try not to laugh, but I have had this desire to write you a poem. Yes, I know I said that I hated poetry, but one of the lads is a poet as well as a teacher, and he's been helping me choose the right words, as well as giving me some tips on other things that poems have. So here it is, DON'T LAUGH!

My love, I need to write,
You know that I must soon go and fight,
My blood for the King I'll give,
My heart in you, will always live,
Should god bring me home,
Our love will be reborn.

Strong I'm sure our children will grow,
They'll believe in hope, I know,
Life may only be short and sweet,
My Annie, I'm sure that we will meet.

There it is. The first poem that I've ever written. I hope you're not embarrassed.
Throw it away, if you are. I'll understand.
Goodbye my love,
I'll write again tomorrow or the next chance I get.

Your loving,

Bill.

So that was what Bill and Boulby were working on. I could hear
Mum and Dad, turning everything off downstairs before coming up
to bed, but I just had to find a letter from Annie and read it before I
could go to sleep.

June 27ᵗʰ 1916,

My sweet Billy,

*I've just read your letter and that beautiful poem. What can I say? I've been
crying so much, that my eyes feel sore. I miss you so very much. Please take care of
yourself.*
*I try to keep myself busy on the farm and the Truswell's spoil me rotten, as
always, but you're the only thing I want. I could live in a cave with you and be
happy. You could go out hunting and I'll take care of the cave and the kids!*
*Anyway, I've written a poem for you now. It's not good, but it's from the heart
and that's all that matters,*

My love, your poem that I've just read,
I must be honest, while in bed,
I spray my perfume lightly, for your love to receive,
That you'll come home, I must believe,
Though you're away now, one day we'll never part,
Please hurry back and help to heal my heart.

I can't wait to see you,
A
XXX

'Bloody hell that was awful!' I said, as I slipped the letter back into the envelope.

Chapter Thirty-One

I woke at nine-thirty, which was much later than I'd been used to, but it was nice to open the curtains and see the familiar row of back gardens. It was even quite comforting to look out over the horrible Mr Webster, who was pottering around his garden next door and no doubt thinking of reasons to be bad tempered. Dad and Mr Webster had fallen out several times about Webster's refusal to return my football when it had gone over onto his flowerbeds. Dad, being such a well-mannered person, had always asked politely for the ball to be returned, only to be faced with a tirade of abuse from Mr Webster, egged on by Webster's equally odious wife. Most of the neighbours hated the couple and ignored them whenever possible. Typically, it was Amanda who made things much worse by dancing around our garden singing a rude song involving the Websters and a tub of glue, which resulted in them going inside their house and not being seen outside for several days.

Mum came into my room, looking anxious, 'Matt… get dressed quickly, the hospital have just called, they want us to get down there as soon as possible. They want to talk to us about Amanda. I knew I should have stayed with her last night, but I wanted to be at home for when you arrived back.'

'Why? What's up mum? Is something wrong?'

'I don't know. They won't say until we get there, so hurry up. Just put any clothes on, it doesn't matter. Come on!'

I dressed hurriedly and without having time to eat any breakfast rushed out to the car, where dad was waiting with the engine running.

No one spoke as we drove through town towards the hospital. Mum was wiping her eyes with a tissue and dad stared blankly ahead as he drove. We parked opposite the hospital and went inside. Mum told the receptionist who we were and why we'd been asked to come down.

'Have a seat and I'll call up and make sure that Doctor Jameel knows that you're here,' said the receptionist as he picked up the receiver.

As we waited, the receptionist had a lengthy conversation on the phone, while all the time looking at us with sympathetic eyes. I tried to occupy myself by looking at people in wheelchairs being pushed past us and away down corridors. I'd spent so much time at the hospital, since Amanda's accident that I had a reasonable medical vocabulary to select from and, could pretend that I was the doctor in charge of directing every incoming patient to the appropriate place.

'Ah yes,' I thought as a boy of around eight or nine years of age was wheeled through some doors opposite us, 'contusion of the cerebral cortex. Get him into theatre immediately! That one needs ten stitches… I say nurse…'

I was part way through a diagnosis when we were approached by a young woman. She smiled at us and said, 'Hi! I'm Doctor Jameel. Thanks for popping down so soon. Please, let's go in here and I'll tell you where we're at.'

'Is Amanda ok?' Mum asked.

We were led into a small and sparsely furnished consulting room where Jameel sat at the table facing us. She took a deep breath and, looking directly at my parents, said, 'There have been… certain changes in Amanda's condition overnight that we thought you needed to know about, before we go up and see her.'

'What kind of changes?' Dad looked worried.

Jameel noticed this and tried to reassure him by saying, 'It's nothing to be worried about as such, but when such changes occur, we have a responsibility to the family of the patient, to explain what they might be. In Amanda's case, we've noticed certain signs that suggest Amanda could be starting to come out of the coma.'

Mum looked across at dad before asking, 'That's good isn't it? So what's changed? Tell us, please!'

'Obviously, any such events are always subtle at first, but overnight Amanda opened her eyes for a few seconds and squeezed the nurse's hand when she called her name. I just don't want us to get carried away by this, because these are early days and any recovery will certainly be a long and slow process. Of course, no one knows if Amanda's brain has sustained any long-term damage, so we must be cautious and not expect too much, too soon.'

'Can we see her now?' said Mum impatiently.

'Of course,' Doctor Jameel said. 'Let's go and see her.'

On the way up to Amanda's room, I hoped, when we got there, that she'd be sitting up in bed asking for an ice cream, but the reality was that she seemed the same as the last time I saw her.

Dad sat next to her and held her hand, 'Hey Amanda, look, Matty's back!'

There was no response, so I held her hand and said, 'Hi, Sis. I've been to see where Bill got his medal.' This time, there was a definite, if small, squeeze on my hand, so I continued, 'And, I saw Our Joe and the other boys.'

Again.

Mum noticed it too and, took Amanda's other hand, saying to me, 'Say something else Matt.'

'Ok… I also saw when Bill and Annie, went to the park and saw the men arguing.'

Two squeezes.

I looked across at mum and smiled, 'I'm sure she knows what I'm talking about Mum.'

I rambled on about some other things I'd seen, but there were no more squeezes and Amanda seemed to have gone away again.

We talked to Amanda for an hour, before Dad said, 'Perhaps she's tired. Let's let her rest and we'll come back later.'

We each kissed Amanda's forehead, before telling her we loved her, and then left.

On the way home, I listened to my parents discussing what had happened and it was clear that they were both trying hard not to become over-optimistic about Amanda's prospects of recovery, while at the same time desperately hoping that the hand squeezes meant something. At one point, Mum said, 'What do you think the squeezes mean, Pete?'

'I don't know,' he answered. 'Obviously, she's responding to something, but I don't want to get carried away. It's my turn to visit her next so I'll try and catch Doctor Jameel and ask her.'

I just kept wondering how Amanda responded when I mentioned Bill and Annie's time together.

Chapter Thirty-Two

The new term at school was only a week away and I had some homework to catch-up with, so I was busy for a couple of days. I knew that had I had to go and see George as soon as possible, but, as a kid, getting in to a nursing home wasn't going to be as simple as it might sound. I would have to get permission first, from my parents, and then The Ferns would have to agree to a visit. Over breakfast with Mum, I decided to start the ball rolling, 'Mum?'

'Yes, Matt. What's up?'

'I want to go and see Mr Spears, at The Ferns.'

'Who's Mr Spears?'

'I've told you about him, Mum. He's the old man who knew Dad's granddad in the war.'

Mum looked puzzled, 'Why do you want to see him?'

'I want to tell him about where I've been and about the graves.'

'Poor old thing. Perhaps he wants to forget about the war. Maybe you should leave him alone and go and play cricket with your mates. Haven't you had enough of the war by now?'

'No, Mum. It's important. Please will you telephone The Ferns and see if I can go and see him. I'll only be a few minutes… promise.'

Mum chewed her toast for a few seconds, before agreeing to my request, 'OK, I'll call later, but I want to get some things done first, like ironing your school uniform, and the garden needs tidying: so you can do that. Remind me, what am I asking for again?'

'I want to call in and see Mr Spears. He knows me.'

Mum was right about being with my mates and when Craig Williams called and asked if I wanted to play cricket with him and some other kids, of course, I couldn't resist. It was close to teatime, before I walked in the house. Dad was sitting in the lounge, watching TV. Without taking his eyes off the screen, he said, 'Your tea's gone cold, Matty. Put the oven on for a few minutes and warm it up if you want.'

'Where's Mum?'

'Visiting Amanda; oh, by the way, apparently you asked her to phone the old folks' home, didn't you?'

'Yes. What did they say?'

'Erm… they said they'd asked My Spears and it's OK for you to go tomorrow about ten. Is that OK?'

'Brilliant dad! Thanks.'

Chapter Thirty-Three

The following morning, I walked through the front door of The Ferns at exactly ten o'clock. No sooner had I stopped, in order to get my bearings, when a voice from behind me said, 'Good morning. Can I help you?'

I turned around and recognised the owner of the voice as being the young man, who had been with George at the school show.

'Hello. I've come to see Mr Spears.'

'Of course. I'm David, and you must be Matthew. Apparently, you're interested in what he did in the war.'

'Yes, that's right.'

'Dear old George, he's such a lovely man. I'm afraid that he's been poorly and gets tired quite quickly these days, so it's best if you don't stay too long. You can always come back to see him another day, he'd love that. He has no family and so no one comes to visit him, which is rather sad. He's usually to be found in the garden on a nice day like today. Please follow me.'

David led me down a corridor and out through some French doors, into the garden. Every one of the elderly people who we passed smiled and seemed pleased to see me. I imagined that many of them hadn't seen a young person in quite some time and I did my best to smile and seem friendly. Eventually, we arrived at a shady corner of the garden, where George was sitting looking out across a lawn. He was so still that I thought that he was asleep, but when he heard us approaching he turned his wheelchair around to face us.

'Hi George, I've got a visitor to see you.'

George was in his familiar blazer and immaculately clean shirt and tie. He shook my hand and said, 'Thanks David, I've been looking forward to seeing Matthew again. He's just come back from the battlefields; did you know he's seen action in the trenches?'

David looked at me and then at George, before smiling patiently and saying that he'd be back in twenty minutes.

George waited until David had left, before speaking again.

'So now you've seen what we went through, all those years ago.'

I told him that I'd had a dream, in which I'd seen everything through Bill's eyes, but that I didn't know if that's what actually happened.

'Did you actually get to the German lines?' I asked.

'You were there and you saw it all. Oh no, it was much more than a dream, because I went back there with you at the same time. Someone or something wanted you to be there and for me to go back, one last time.'

'I don't understand.'

'Neither do I, but as soon as I knew who you are, I had this feeling that we'd make that journey together. Those boys who died deserve to be remembered for who there were and what they did. Now you've met them and spent time with them, perhaps you're the person to tell other people about them. The sad thing is that all people ever see of them, are monuments with their names carved on them or their gravestones, and once a year we wear poppies for a week or so, before forgetting them again.'

'That's very sad, George.'

'Yes, it is. Have you got any questions for me, before I go?'

'Where are you going?'

'I'll be off to meet Bill, Joe and the others before long.'

'Did you see Bill much after the war?'

'Oh yes, from time to time, but he'd got Annie and his family, and my life sort of went in another direction. I went to live and work in Derby and we only saw each other at regimental reunions or if I happened to be back in Sheffield. I never married; there was only really one lass who I would have asked to marry me, but someone else got there before me... Ah well. Anyway I ended up owning a few newsagents shops in Derby, until I retired and eventually washed up in here.'

'Do you know what happened to Boulby?'

'I heard that he struggled after the war, but I'm not sure where he ended up.'

'That's very sad.'

'It is, isn't it, but I can understand why. We tried to rebuild our lives, but the war took something away from us that we never got back again, if you know what I mean. I'm sure I heard someone say that the war made our colours run dry, which sounds right somehow. Anyway, twenty years later, many of the boys were ready to fight again, but by then we were a bit too old and they gave us other things to do instead. We were spent.'

David appeared from behind some rose bushes and said that I had to go now, because it was time for George to have his mid-morning cup of tea and that he needed a rest, so I left with the promise that I would come back again.

Chapter Thirty-Four

School work and Amanda's well-being, took up most of my time and it was autumn before I got a chance to go and visit The Ferns again. Much to my surprise, Dad asked if he could come with me.

'I'd like to come. I sense that he'd like me to be there,' Dad said.

When we got there, things had changed.

George was now bedridden and very weak. David stirred George from his drowsiness, to tell him that he'd got visitors.

'George,' I said quietly. 'I've brought my dad. Is that all right?'

'Of course,' George said. 'It's nice of you to come as see me. Tell me Mathew, have you studied our war at school?'

'No, not yet, George. We're doing the Romans in history at the moment.'

'That's a pity,' he said sadly, 'but perhaps you'll study it soon, eh?'

'Oh yes. I know we're going to be learning about it soon.'

I was lying of course, but I couldn't leave him without giving him some hope that he and the Sheffield lads would be remembered in some way.

We fell into silence for a few minutes, during which George looked away into the distance, and I thought that he was going to fall asleep. Dad and I exchanged worried glances, as George seemed to have gone into a trance, but instead of drifting away he became more lucid and his voice grew stronger.

'Are you both still there?' said George at last.

'Yes, George.' I replied. 'Can I get anything for you?

'No, I'm fine, thank you. Do you know much about Bill's life in the months and years after the war?'

'I'd very much like to know, if it's Ok,' Dad answered.

'Well… I think that if I don't tell you now, then it might soon be too late.

'So, when it was over, and all of us who survived the war came home to our friends and families, it was really hard for a lot of lads to just settle down into normal life again. I was quite lucky, but Bill struggled. In my day, we used to call what he had, "shell shock." For a few years, after the war ended, Bill used to have some terrible dreams about being back in battle and he'd wake up crying and screaming. Some days Bill was very hard to live with and not the bloke he used to be. He'd sometimes be quite unpleasant, particularly when he'd had a drink or two.'

'That's horrible,' I said.

'Yes, it was and Annie found it really difficult. In fact, one time, she went off to stay with her mother, until Bill had sorted himself out. I used to call around to see her at her mother's house, in order to check that she was coping. I'd got a car by then, and sometimes I'd take her out for a drive into the countryside. I suppose I was keeping my promise to Bill to look after Annie, while he was away.'

'That was very kind of you... George, are you OK?'

George seemed to be struggling to breathe and I thought of calling David, but after a short time he regained his composure,

'Yes, yes, I'm fine. I was just remembering something, that's all.'

'What can you remember?'

'You'll find out, Matthew: that when two adults become very close, things can sometimes go too far and they end up doing things that they both regret.'

'What do you mean?' I was, by now, struggling to understand where this was all going. Dad stayed quiet and let the old man finish his story.

'I mean that I once told Annie that she should have married me and not Bill. Well, after that, she got upset and we sort of fell out. She went back to Bill and that was that. The last time I saw Annie was on one afternoon when I called around to say that I was moving away. Bill was at work and we talked about some good times that we'd had through the years and I was on my way.'

'That's very sad, George.'

'Yes, it is... Anyway, Bill sorted himself out and they became a family when the boy was born. Becoming a dad, helped Bill to get his life back together and I was very happy for them. Now if you don't mind, I'd like to have a sleep now. Come and see me as soon as you can... promise?'

'I promise,' I said.

George died on the following Thursday.

Dad wouldn't let me go to George's funeral. He said that someone of my age shouldn't go to a funeral, because: 'Life's full of sadness as it is, and you'll be going to plenty of them as you go through life.'

I was very upset at the time, but, looking back, I understand what he meant. Dad had no idea that I'd already seen as much death as him.

Chapter Thirty-Five

We'd been warned by the doctors that Amanda's recovery would take time and they were right. With every passing week there was some sign of improvement, which was usually followed by one of disappointment. Mum had allowed herself to become overly optimistic that Amanda might even be home soon, but her hopes were dashed when Amanda developed an infection and sank back into her seemingly endless sleep.

Happily, the direction of Amanda's recovery remained in the right direction and by the following spring she was semi-conscious and starting to recognise us. Dad played her some tunes on the ukulele and Mum talked to her about Paul McCartney. By the end of May, arrangements had been made for Amanda to come home to complete her recovery with her family around her.

Mum and Dad set to work redecorating Amanda's bedroom and getting the house as clean as possible. Amanda's favourite teddy bear was placed on her bed and all of her treasures were positioned where she could find them. One or two of the neighbours (not the Websters) brought cakes and presents for Amanda and even the local newspaper sent someone to interview us. Eventually, the big day arrived and an ambulance pulled up outside our house.

Amanda emerged from the ambulance, smiling and blinking in the bright sunlight. She would still need physiotherapy to help her walk again, but there she was, home and back among us again. We'd been told that her speech might be slow to return, but that, if we talked to her as much as possible, it would encourage her to find her voice. This turned out to be the case and over several more months she was able to communicate nearly as well as she had ever done.

One Sunday afternoon, when I got back after having been on my bike, I found Amanda sitting alone in her deck chair, watching a care-free butterfly flitting between the flowers. She turned to me and held out her arms for a hug. After we'd embraced, she looked at me and said, 'Did you enjoy meeting Bill and Annie? You know how Bill got his medal, don't you?'

'How do you know so much about what happened?'

'I arranged it all for you. You don't think I was just lying there asleep all that time, do you?'

'I don't understand. Are you joking?'

'It's all a bit complicated, but let's just say that I had the chance to visit... the room next door... you know, where we go when we die, but I decided not to stay. Anyway, while I was there, I asked Bill to help me plan a surprise for you.'

'So, all of this was down to you?'

'Yes. Did you like it?'

I was waiting for the familiar Amanda giggle: like the one she has when she's been mischievous, but it didn't happen. She seemed totally serious. I said that the most important thing was to have my sister back and that I would have gone without any of it, if it would have helped her. She put her arms around me again and said, 'Well, I'm back. Let's make the most of what time we have, while we can. Incidentally, I hope that you don't think that you've learned all that there is to know. I suspect that there are more surprises waiting for you, even if I'm not around.'

Chapter Thirty-Six

I did well at school, particularly in history, and, after getting decent grades in my A-levels, I decided to study at a higher level and go to university. History was always my passion, and in July 1980, I was offered a place at a university, to study history and politics.

Amanda was happy and had enrolled on a course at an Art college in Sheffield. While she still lived with mum and dad, she had learned to manage her health problems and had made some very good friends who understood her needs, and supported her whenever she needed them.

Life at university suited me perfectly, and I was also able to quickly make friends and had got into both the cricket and football teams. I was committed to my studies and to having as much fun as possible. In fact, I saw nothing ahead of me but endless pleasure.

February 1982 was a particularly cold, and I often had to trudge some miles in deep snow from my room in a hall of residence to the lecture theatre on the main university campus. Some of my friends stayed in bed, rather than make the effort, but I cared enough to want to do well in my exams.

On my way to lectures I sometimes called into the Student's Union, in order to check my pigeonhole for any messages or letters from home. On this particular day, there was a note asking me to call home urgently. So, I fumbled in my pocket for some coins and went into one of the telephone booths.

Dad answered the phone and, from the tone of his voice, I knew that something was badly wrong. I could hear Mum crying in the background.

'What's up, Dad?'

'Matty, Amanda died this morning.'

'Mum tried to wake her up and… '

'Oh no!' I gripped the telephone receiver tightly. 'I'll be home as soon as I can.'

Someone gave me a lift into town and I managed to get the last ticket on a coach, leaving at three in the afternoon. Road closures, due to the weather, meant that I didn't arrive home until late in the evening. Dad took my hand and led me through into the front room. We sat quietly, asking ourselves why Amanda had to be taken from us. Mum barely spoke as she cradled Amanda's teddy bear and sobbed.

News travels quickly and, by the time we came downstairs in the morning, several sympathy cards had already been pushed through the letterbox. Mum opened each one and cried at the messages they contained.

Once the formalities as to the cause of Amanda's death were over (the official verdict was death by natural causes due to an epileptic seizure) we were able to arrange a funeral and start to build a life without her. I took a month off university, and spring was in the air when I returned to my studies.

My friends did their best to help me by arranging nights out to the cinema and other pleasant gatherings, but the loss of my sister had hit me hard. Getting to sleep at night was especially difficult, and, when it came, it was preceded by several hours of restless stirring and replaying of the many happy times we'd shared. She seemed to be everywhere and I could often hear Amanda's laughter echoing through my mind, as clearly as it always had ever done. While I loved to hear her again, every call of "Matty look out!" or "Matty, sing me a Beatles song" reverberated through my mind and forced me to confront her loss once more. I was restless and I sensed that, somehow, Amanda had not yet found her own peace. It was as if she needed to stay with me until some task had been completed, or some message had been conveyed to someone. On one occasion I was sitting in a lecture theatre, attempting to find some interest in a presentation by Professor Garson on the role of dung in medieval society, when I found myself being consumed with grief and with tears running down my cheeks.

'Was Garson's lecture really that bad?' someone asked me later.

After several weeks of restlessness and more lectures the term ended and I boarded a coach back home, in the hope that I'd be able to get some sleep in my faithful old bed. I was even looking forward to seeing the Websters again. If only I could somehow let Amanda go

As a student, spending money was limited, and rather than buying the necessary books that had been recommended for my studies, I would sometimes go into town and see if they were in the

Central Library on Surrey Street. Having failed to obtain a copy of a particular book I was walking through the city centre, when I came across a line of people standing at a bus stop. The bus pulled up next to me and, with pneumatic wheeze, its doors opened and the line of, largely elderly, people began to climb on board. Such was the eagerness of the would-be passengers to get on the bus, that I stepped aside and let them file past me as I walked around them. As I looked back at the bus, the sign on the front read: 52a Loxley. The last passenger was now on board and handing over his fare to the driver when something made me turn around and get on the bus. The problem was that now I was facing the rather large and impatient looking driver without any clue as to where I wanted to go. I'd never been to Loxley on a bus and I had no idea as to what to say.

'Where to?' said the stomach.

I hesitated, for what felt like an hour, before blurting out, 'Loxley, please.'

'Well, that's a shock. Where about *in* Loxley do you want to be?' I mean, there's old Loxley, or Loxley Bottom or Loxley Hill. Which one? I really wouldn't want you to get off at the wrong stop!'

The driver's sarcasm seemed to amuse him and he smiled contentedly as he waited for an answer. By now I became aware of the rows of impatient passengers, who were now obviously becoming restless and eager for their journey to begin.

'Loxley Hill, please,' I said, eventually.

'Are you quite sure?' asked the driver, with mock concern.

'Yes, I am,' I said, wishing to be invisible.

'That's twenty pence, please. If you're not sure where to get off, look out for a very steep hill. You know what a hill is, don't you?'

Averting my eyes from his artificially sickly smile, I placed twenty pence on to the metal cash tray, before taking my ticket and finding a seat at the back of the bus, still unsure as to what to do when I got there.

The journey took the bus along one of the main roads on the edge of town, past the Sheffield Wednesday ground, before turning left and climbing up a steep hill, past rows of terraced houses. A voice in my head said.

'This is probably Loxley Hill.'

'Wow! You're so perceptive!' answered another part of my brain.

By the time that the bus had crawled up the hill most of the other passengers had got off at the various bus stops on the way up, and I must have cut a rather anxious and lonely figure, sitting on my own on the back seat, wondering where to get off. I noticed that as the hill levelled out the scene outside was becoming more agricultural and we were passing open fields, some with grazing cattle. Not wanting to find myself stranded somewhere in the countryside, I pressed the stop button and got off.

The bus left in a cloud of blue diesel smoke and I looked around, already starting to wonder what had made me make this journey. Well, at least the views across the open fields from a farm gate were nice, and, somewhat unexpectedly, a horse came over to a gate and nuzzled up to me, no doubt interested in whether I had any treats to give it. I've never been much of an animal person, but I quite enjoyed stroking it, and, much to the horse's surprise as well as mine, I found a half-open packet of sweets in my pocket, which we shared.

'You're quite a nice horse aren't you?' I said, and the horse seemed to understand what I meant as it helped itself to another mint imperial.

After a few minutes, our brief relationship ended when the horse became bored with me and wandered over to where another horse was involved in something more interesting than taking sweets from a puzzled looking human.

With a view to catching the next bus back to the city centre, I crossed the road and looked up and down for the nearest bus stop. That's when I became aware of a large sign, heralding the imminent construction of a new development on some land behind the wall. I would normally pay no attention to anything like this, as I was likely to be years away from ever being interested in buying a house. This was different. In large red lettering and with apparent pride, it heralded the arrival of:

TRUSWELL COURT.
MODERN LIVING ON THE EDGE OF THE CITY.
A RANGE OF TWO, THREE AND FOUR
BEDROOMED DWELLINGS.
FOR DETAILS, CONTACT OUR SALES TEAM ON
0114 2485846.

Beneath, there were some artist impressions of what these houses would look like. They showed happy people cleaning their cars on the drive of a sparkly modern house, while others chatted with their neighbours and patted the dog.

'Truswell Court. Truswell Court.' I found myself repeating this, perhaps rather too loudly and I looked around in the hope that no one was around to hear me apparently mumbling to myself and starting to become visibly excited.

The soon to be Truswell Court was still at that time an overgrown scattering of empty and seemingly derelict farm buildings around a farmyard. I stood at the gate, looking at the farm buildings and imagined Bill struggling to leave Annie behind, as he went off to war. This was where it all happened. These fields must have been where they walked and talked on Annie's day off from the farm. It was from this gate, that Mrs Truswell led Annie back inside, as Bill made his way down the hill.

The cacophony arrived and Bill's voice emerged.

Chapter Thirty-Seven

You're a grown man now, Matthew, and you deserve to have the answer to some questions. I had planned to leave things as they are, but… let's put it like this… a new voice has come into the picture and she is very keen that I should share the rest of my story with you.

I knew who he was talking about. Bill continued.

I found myself de-mobbed from the army and desperate to see Annie again. I thought we'd pick up where we left off, but I'd come home a changed bloke. I had no confidence in myself to do even the basic things properly. For reasons that I can't explain, I started to blame myself for Joe's death and for many others,' as well. I went back to work at Gibbs, but I'd go out on a Saturday morning and stay out all day, either drinking with strangers or walking aimlessly for mile after mile, before coming home in the early hours of the morning. Annie tried her best to help, but I pushed away and so she went to her mum's for a while, leaving me to try and sort myself out.

This went on for several months. She'd sometimes come home and then I'd be unkind to her, and then she'd leave again. I really had no one to talk to and I could see no way out of my pain.

One Friday afternoon I clocked off work early, having told the boss that I needed to go somewhere urgently. My plan had been to find a pub and have a couple of pints. I thought I'd try the Hangingwater Arms in Wadsley, as it was on the way home. The pub could be reached either by going the long way through the housing estate or by taking a short cut across some fields and through the cemetery. Given how thirsty I was, cutting through the graveyard was the obvious way of getting there.

Almost as soon as I stepped through the green, wrought iron gates, I could hear something that sounded like nothing I'd ever come across before. There were wolf-like howls, interspersed with what sounded like cries of agony. Whatever the creature was, its misery must have been complete and absolute. It was only when I reached the end of a row of large Victorian monuments that I saw what had been making all this noise.

He had his back to a gravestone and was facing away from me, so that I could only see the top of his head over the top. Even then, I recognised the shape of his head and his fine wispy hair.

I walked around the grave and faced him. Boulby's eyes were closed and in his hand was a half-empty bottle of whisky. His face was now sallow and weather-beaten and his clothes, close to being rags, were hanging from an emaciated frame. I thought of how he'd always been so fastidious about cleanliness, even when living below ground.

'Boulby. It's me Bill. You remember me, Bill Farrell?' I said. 'We served together.'

Boulby opened his eyes and his face formed into a sneer of contempt; his eyes laden with sadness.

'No. I haven't served anyone,' he answered. 'I've put on a uniform and done a bit of marching around and charging across a wasteland, but I haven't *served* anyone.'

'Yes you have. You're one of the Pals. You volunteered, just like I did.'

'To hell with the Pals. To hell with the king. Who did you say you were? I don't remember you from anywhere and if it's money you want, I haven't got any.'

'I don't want your money, Boulby.'

'What do you want then?'

'I don't know. I was walking through here and I could hear someone's voice. I had no idea that it was you, until just now. So what are you doing here?'

Boulby began to laugh and his laughter echoed among the mouldering dead around us, 'I live here. This is my home. I look after Kenneth.'

Boulby shifted to one side and, I could now see what was carved into the gravestone behind him. It read:

Kenneth Thackeray Hornby
1890-1918,
Time shall not keep us apart.

Boulby turned to face the grave and said, 'Kenneth, look who's here? It's... who did you say you are again?'

'Bill Farrell.'

'No, I don't know who he is either, but let's humour him shall we? Yes, me too.'

Then turning to face me, he began to wave his finger in the direction of some trees around the edge of the cemetery.

'That's my home over there, those trees. Nice aren't they? I've got a lovely little tent in there. Nice fire in winter, perfect. Now leave me alone.'

I felt compelled to ask the obvious question, while not holding out much hope of a sensible answer.

'Who was Kenneth?' I asked.

'Ah now, that's a good question. Who was Kenneth? You mean who *is* Kenneth; he's still here, can't you see him?'

He took a long drink out of the bottle and continued, 'My Kenneth was an officer in the Devonshires over in France. After that shambles of a battle, someone decided that I was a loony and they put me in hospital. That's where we met. They'd sent him in there, but, just like me, he was perfectly fine.'

Boulby lost his train of thought for a few seconds, before remembering what he'd been telling me, 'Kenneth and I shared the same views on art and poetry, and he asked me to come and live with him in Warminster. Then, guess what? The little devil went and died, so I brought him back here to be close to me.'

'I'm sorry, Boulby.'

'Oh, it's fine, don't you worry about me. You can go now. Cheerybye, Bob!'

'Let me help you,' I said, without any real idea as to how I might do it,

'Before you go,' said Boulby, 'answer me this. Have you a wife? A girlfriend? Someone special to you? Y'know someone who gives a damn about you?'

'Yes. I have.'

'Then go home, whoever you are. Be nice to him or her. Make the best of what time you have together, Mr Soldier. Now if you'll excuse me, I feel a song coming on.'

After another long drink, Boulby began to sing again and send his wolf-like howls across the churchyard.

Chapter Thirty-Eight

On the following morning, I was up early and was at the door of Mrs Parker by nine-thirty. Annie's mother opened the door and looked genuinely shocked to see me.

'Is Annie in?' I asked,

'She's not here, Bill. George Spears called earlier and they've gone out in his car for the day. I think they were going for a drive and a picnic somewhere. Do you want to come in for a cup of tea?'

I tried to pretend that Annie had told me about her plans for the day and that I'd forgotten.

'Of course,' I said. 'My mistake. Anyway, would you tell her that I called and that I need to talk to her?'

Mrs Parker could see right through my effort to seem nonchalant.

'I think you'd better come in, Bill. It's you and I who need to talk.'

I followed her in and she gestured for me to sit down on the settee and she sat in the armchair, opposite me.

'Now what's going on with you two? Be honest with me.'

I told Mrs Parker that I had been struggling to adjust to life outside of the army and that Annie had borne the brunt of my frequent bad moods and excessive drinking. I told her what I'd seen and how I felt guilty at having survived when so many lads had fallen around me. I said that even in the dark of the night the thought of Annie got me through until morning.

'Perhaps it might have been better if I'd been killed.'

'Don't be so silly,' she snapped. 'I know dozens of women who've lost their men in one way or another, either in battle, or like I did. You're just being bloody selfish now. You know, when Annie told me about you, I immediately thought that you were far too young to marry, but it soon became clear that you adored each other and that you should be together. After she'd met you Annie changed from being a rather soppy girl into a beautiful young woman. That was down to you.'

'I love her as much as I ever have done,' I said, fighting back tears.

Annie's mother listened intently and leaned towards me. 'She feels the same way about you, but you haven't made it easy for her lately. Have you?'

'No… and I'm sorry. What can I do?'

'Talk to her. Tell her how you feel and don't just shut yourself off. That's not healthy for your marriage. She married you for what you are and what you'll be. True love doesn't change when people change, it adapts and grows with the years.'

'I thought that I was protecting her by not sharing my thoughts with her.'

'Wrong, wrong, wrong. That's not how it should be. I'll talk to her and I'll tell her that we've had a chat.'

'What are you going to say to her?' I asked.

'I'm going to tell her that she should go home and that you'll talk to her and let her help you, in the way that she wants to. Is that what you'll do?'

'Yes.'

'That's the best news she could have. Now, do you want another cup of tea?'

Chapter Thirty-Nine

A soon as I walked through the door I set about tidying the cottage, in as far as I knew what that meant. Not that the house needed much doing to it, as Annie had always made sure that everything was clean and tidy. She told me that, on occasions, she and Mrs Truswell would take an hour off work and chat over a cup of tea, so Annie would make sure that the place looked at its best. I had picked some wild flowers from a nearby meadow and placed them in a vase on the window ledge. Annie always loved wild flowers.

At around six o'clock, the door opened and Annie walked through into the living room. She stopped in her tracks when she saw me standing there.

'I'm sorry,' I said. 'I've been an idiot and I should have been more honest with you about how I've been feeling. Please forgive me.'

Annie said nothing and walked to the window, gazing out towards the stables. She remained there for several minutes, before turning to face me, 'What's changed Bill?'

I told her that I'd been thinking a lot about how I'd treated her since I came home and that our marriage was the only thing that really mattered. After I'd said all this, I could see that she was still sceptical,

'But what exactly has happened to bring this about. I want my Bill back, not this moody and unhappy ghost of a man. How come you've changed so much and others who were in the army haven't changed at all?'

'You mean George?'

'Yes, George. He's been more of a friend to me than you've been lately.'

'George is doing what I asked him to do.'

'What's that mean?'

'I asked him to take care of you if I didn't come home, and I guess that's what he's been doing. In a sort of way, I suppose some of me didn't come home. He's always loved you, but you know that.'

'Stop it!'

'Come on Annie. Don't be silly. It's been obvious. Anyway, I'm going to work as hard as I can to make it up to you. I love you more than he could ever do and I'm begging you to give me another chance.'

'You still haven't answered my question about what's changed you.' She was not going to let anything go until she knew what had brought about this change in me.

I told her about meeting Boulby and my conversation with her mother. A smile came across Annie's face as I recounted what her mum had said to me.

'My mother! She's not daft is she? Never underestimate her, because she knows me as well as anyone and we've talked a lot over recent months, especially when you've gone on one of your funny turns. Give us a kiss then and promise me that you'll start to tell me when you're struggling!'

I told her that I would and that I would try to fight the darkness, which on occasions had taken over my mind. I said that the best way to remember Our Joe was to try and live my life to the full and to take care of my family.

This is what I did. Our son arrived on one freezing afternoon in December and that changed everything. The idea of becoming a father had never really seemed like something that could happen to me, yet there I was cradling him with his blue eyes and dark curly hair.

Those first years were tough, and on many occasions I faced the prospect of losing my job, but somehow Gibbs survived and I was eventually promoted to foreman, which brought a welcome increase in pay. Annie continued to work on the farm and the Truswells remained our greatest friends.

Our son, Stuart, grew into a tall and athletic boy, talented in cricket and football. I bought an old car and we'd go out as a family into Derbyshire and have picnics. If there happened to be a football match nearby Stuart would want to watch it and he'd want to discuss every possible aspect of tactics and technique. Annie would have liked a daughter, but that never happened.

Stuart would sometimes ask me about my time in the army, but I was always reluctant to talk about it. I gave him a broad outline of my time on the Somme and about his uncle Joe, but it was a chapter in my life that I was unwilling to reopen. I certainly never mentioned the medal. I kept it in a box somewhere at the back of my wardrobe and I certainly never wore it, even at reunions or on Armistice Day. To me, it represented a time of pain and suffering, for a cause that was still unclear. Most of all, it reminded me of all the lads who were lost out there and especially Joe.

Stuart left school at fourteen and started work on the farm. Mr Truswell had been unwell for some time and so he needed extra labour to keep things going. One evening in the summer of 1936 we'd just finished tea, when I noticed that Stuart seemed to be more interested in looking out of the window than what I had been talking about. At around seven, he announced that he felt like taking a walk over the fields and getting some fresh air. Annie asked him if he wanted her to come with him, but he said he'd be fine and that he wouldn't be long. Neither of us thought anything of it; after all, it was a lovely evening and he'd worked hard all day, so going for a walk seemed perfectly normal. Stuart took a walk on the following evening and the next one (despite the heavy rain) and it was only then that I began to wonder if he was meeting someone.

The question was answered a week later when Stuart came home with Ruth, and, from then, other than during the working hours, they were inseparable. Ruth was the daughter of Walter Burns, a neighbouring farmer, and his late wife Enid. Rather like Annie had done to me, she had completely captured Stuart's heart. Ruth was a pretty and kind girl and she fitted seamlessly into our family. Somehow, it seemed inevitable that she and Stuart, despite being so young, would want to marry as soon as possible. Of course, they faced the same spectre of war, just as Annie and I had done. Stuart had expressed a desire, like I had, to join up and "do his bit." I tried my best to dissuade him, but his mind was set on joining the RAF and, that was it. Stuart was determined to fight Hitler and would join up as soon as he was able to do so.

First, however, came their marriage, which was organised almost completely by Ruth's family, although Annie and I paid our share of the costs. At the age of eighteen, Stuart found himself married, with a child on the way. To add to their burden, the "one" child, turned out to be twins (a girl and a boy), and, had Ruth's father, not built an extension to their house, then these young parents would have struggled for somewhere to live. As it was, Stuart, Ruth and the children, settled in to a life over at High Lodge Farm.

Annie and I would often look after the twins in order to give Stuart and Ruth a break and we loved to see them whenever possible. Their little boy, Peter, was the image of his father and I always thought his twin sister, Jenny, was so much like Annie, with the same hazel eyes and beguiling smile. Both were happy and healthy children. That changed on one morning in April 1940.

Chapter Forty

I remember hearing the downstairs clock strike three and, shortly afterwards, someone began to hammer at our front door. There were screams and shouts coming from outside and my first thought was that someone had burgled the farmhouse. The horses had become agitated and were rattling their chains and stamping their feet. Whatever had happened, it was obviously serious and I was out of bed and downstairs in moments.

I opened the door, to find Walter, looking deathly pale and seemingly having trouble standing up.

'It's Ruth and Stuart!' was all he could say.

'Why, what's happened? Tell me!'

'There's been an accident Bill, you need to come.'

That night was worse than any I'd had before. Honestly, Matthew, I'd have gone through the Somme again, rather than experience what happened. It's probably too much to describe in detail now, except to say that Stuart and Ruth died after being hit by a car, driven by a drunk driver. We laid them to rest together in Loxley Cemetery.

For the sake of the twins, Annie and I dug deeply into our reserves of strength and took on the job of raising the little ones. Walter tried to do his bit, but without Enid by his side and with a farm to run, it seemed natural for Annie and me to adopt them and give them a chance in life. The war raged on and I joined the Home Guard. I recall racing down to the city centre on the night of the blitz, to try and help out in some way. The city survived and we rebuilt our shattered streets.

Annie started to become unwell in the early 1950s and, despite that, because she loved those children with all her heart, she never showed any sign of slowing down, even right to the end. I tried to hang on without her, but my time came, not long after hers.

I don't know if your dad ever mentions us, but I hope that he remembers us fondly. There is still much for you to find and discover about your past, so take your time and think about where you came from and what you want to achieve. Above all, try to be the best person that you can be and make the best of the talents that you have. This is the end of my time with you for now, although I suspect we will meet again. Never forget my generation and those who did not come home.

Bill's voice faded away and was replaced by birdsong.

Chapter Forty-One

I opened the gate and started to make my way towards the farmhouses. I suppose that I'd gone twenty metres down the gravel drive, when someone called, 'Excuse me. Can I help you?'

I turned sharply in the direction of where the voice had come, to see a man approaching me from one of the buildings, where he'd been throwing things into a skip.

'Yes. I'm sorry to bother you.' I said, trying not to seem too afraid, 'I… was just passing and I thought that I'd have a look around.'

'This is private property. Didn't you see the "Keep Out" signs? Are you blind?'

'No, it's just that my great-granddad lived here and I wanted to see what it was like before they knock it down. I'll go. I'm sorry I only wanted to see what it was like.'

'There's not much to see here, son, only a few knackered old farmhouses. Me and the lads are gutting them before we start demolition tomorrow, so I'd be off, if I was you.'

'Please can I just have a look? I'll only be a minute. I won't touch anything.'

'Well… I suppose it can't hurt… Just five minutes.'

'Thanks. If you want to watch me, then I don't mind.'

The man seemed slightly more convinced of my honesty by now and there was a hint of a smile on his face, 'I've got to finish clearing out all this rubbish and I'm a bit behind. Go and have a look if you want, but there's nothing left now. We've thrown all the stuff we found into skips and taken most of it away. There's only this one left and that's going later today. The farmhouse is obviously where the Truswells lived and the farm workers lived in the others. The Lansleys lived in the one over there and I'm pretty sure the Farrells had the one across the yard.'

He turned and walked back towards the farmhouse, whistling *She Loves You.*

He was right. Each building was now no more than an empty

shell and as I stood peering through the darkness into the Farrell's cottage, I tried to imagine what each room might have been. I could see that one room still had a fireplace and that another space had to have been the kitchen. Soon it would all be gone, and more traces of Farrell's lives with it.

I turned away, feeling that this was as far as I was going to go in my search for Bill and Annie.

'Cheers! Thanks for letting me have a look,' I called in the direction of the skip.

The whistling had stopped and no one answered, so I assumed that the man had gone around the back of the building and couldn't hear me. Perhaps he was inside. Either way, I wanted him to see that I'd gone, so I thought that it wouldn't hurt to find him.

'Hello! Are you there?'

Silence.

I followed a path towards the back of the buildings, still expecting to see him, but there was no sign of anyone having been there. Tentatively, I made my way to the door of the farmhouse and called into the emptiness. Again, there was no response, only the creaking of the rotting timbers in the breeze. The house had no staircase remaining, so anyone in there had to have been a ground level, yet still there was no one around.

I supposed that he could have gone to the shop or perhaps, as there was no toilet on site, he might have had gone into the bushes, but it seemed odd that he'd just disappeared so quickly without telling me; after all, I'd only been looking at the cottage for a minute or two. I wondered where the others had gone. He said that "the lads" were working here, but I'd seen no sign of anyone else but him.

Before I left, I decided that it wouldn't hurt anyone, if I had a look at what he'd been throwing into the skip, so I lifted one or two things up and looked inside. It seemed to be mainly broken furniture and a few broken photograph frames (each without a photograph) but nothing that seemed to be of any value. In fact, the only thing that I could see in there, of any interest was a metal container, about the size of a cereal box, which, other than a few scratches, appeared to be undamaged.

I reached in and having moved some rather stinky old stuff to one side, I was able to bring the box to the surface to have a closer look at it. I could hear something rattling around, inside the box, but the lid was locked. Carefully, having wiped away some of the greasy dirt, I slipped the box into my rucksack and started to make my way down the drive, towards the main Loxley road. That's when a yellow van turned up the drive towards me, making it almost impossible for me to get past it.

Three men were sitting in the front seats of the van and two of them got out, leaving only the driver inside. The largest one of the two moved towards me. He was a giant of a man, with a bushy beard and wild hair. I couldn't help noticing how his fists were clenching and how his huge biceps were starting to flex in his bare arms.

'What are you up to?' he snarled, with eyes seemingly intent on dismantling my body for fun.

'Nothing. Nothing. Honestly,' I stammered.

'So what are you doing in here? Are you after nicking some stone from the site? 'cos if you are… '

'Stone? No. I was just doing some research into my family history. Your mate, up there, said that it was OK for me to have a look around. Ask him… he'll tell you.'

I thought that referring to the other man as his "mate" might give the impression that I was somehow on his side in all matters of the world and therefore I might be less likely to come to serious physical harm.

'What the bloody hell are you on about? We've come here to work on this site and there's nobody else working on here today.'

He lunged towards me, his tattoos glistening with sweat and menacing intent, causing me to fall back into the hedge.

'Leave him, Bonzo!' Shouted the driver through the open window of the van. 'Look at him. Let him go, we've still got loads to do before we knock off.'

The beast stepped grudgingly to one side, muttering something under his breath, which I assumed related to his ongoing desire to dismember me, and I was able to squeeze past the van into the safety of the "non-Bonzo" universe. Roars of laughter came from the van as I made my way down the drive, still trembling, to the bus stop.

Chapter Forty-Two

Once home, I raided Dad's toolbox for something that might force off the lid of the metal box. The lid seemed reluctant to come off and it took half an hour of strenuous levering with a screwdriver (accompanied by some swearing) before it surrendered its secrets.

Inside, were a few faded envelopes and a small parcel wrapped in yellowing muslin, tied up with string. With all the care of an archaeologist gently unveiling the secrets of some long lost tomb, I peeled back the folds of cloth and, before I could process all of this, Bill's medal lay in the palm of my hand.

Though it was dirty, on the face of the silver circular medal, I could still see the head of King Edward VII and on the other side the inscription FOR BRAVERY IN THE FIELD, surrounded by a laurel wreath. The ribbon was dark blue, with red and white stripes running vertically down. Hurriedly, I wiped the medal down and the face of the medal returned to something like it must have been.

Bill's hand had been the last one to touch it this and here it was: a relic of an act of courage, long ago, by a man who would rather have not won it at all, in a war that was totally avoidable. It seemed that the picture of Bill's life was now complete and my attention turned to the letters. They were, I imagined, more letters between Bill and Annie and, the first few were exactly that. One envelope contained a clipping from a local newspaper, reporting on the death of Stuart and Ruth. Once again, I thought of Bill's emotions as he placed this in the box. Had he been here now, Dad would have probably become emotional again and I would have looked away, to avoid embarrassing him.

I was about to put all these things back into the box, when I noticed that one envelope seemed to want me to open it first. The handwriting on it, was neither that of Bill or Annie, yet it seemed tantalisingly familiar and I knew I'd seen it many times before. The shapes of the M and the Y were that of someone I had known. The envelope was sealed and, in my eagerness to get to the letter, I tore it open.

Dear Matty,

I dropped this into the box, just before Bill buried it, so he doesn't know it's in here. I'll be in trouble now, wont I?

I wanted to tell you that I love you and that I'll always be with you. In fact, I've already been with the family for many years already, either as Amanda and one or two other people that you've known. I'll let you guess who else I've been!

My trips into your world bring me into the lives of many people, but being your sister was my favourite one by far. I'm sorry that I left you all so suddenly, but that's how it is sometimes.

Arranging for you to meet Bill and Annie was just wonderful and I was watching you the whole time, from my hospital bed!

Take Bill's medal and the gifts that are still to come and do great things. I'm never far from your side on the long and winding road and may smiles awake you when you rise.

Amanda

References

The First and Last of the Sheffield City Battalion by John Cornwell.

Redmires: Tales from the Ridge by Keith Baker.

Acknowledgements

With thanks to Steven Kay of 1889 publishing, for his unending support and endless patience.

Thanks also to Vanessa Ward, for her invaluable input and of course to my family for tolerating my grumpiness during its creation.

This novel is dedicated to my cousin, Ian Boulby, who shares my love and respect for our Grandfather and who has unearthed much of what we know about his experiences of World War One. Thanks for the medal, Ian!

The greatest thanks is to the Sheffield Pals and to all those who have made the ultimate sacrifice in the service of this nation.

www.ingramcontent.com/pod-product-compliance
Lightning Source LLC
Chambersburg PA
CBHW010545170726
48285CB00008B/2756